thor

D1715696

The Group Home

A work of fiction in which
the truth can be told

The Group Home

*A work of fiction in which
the truth can be told*

David Seila

Michael Skubal

Published by
HenschelHAUS Publishing, Inc.
www.henschelhausbooks.com

Hardcover ISBN: 978159598-481-4
Paperback ISBN: 978159598-482-1
E-ISBN: 978159598-490-6
Audio book: 978159598-502-6
Library of Congress Number: 2016951076

Cover design and author photos by Chris Mattison

Printed in the United States of America

A portion of the proceeds from the sale of this book will be donated to the group home.

This book is dedicated to the Group Home
and the individuals who chose to learn
from their experiences working there.

To Mr. Mark, for unwavering dedication to the kids,
and for always showing up with a positive attitude and
compassion for people I rarely see.

To Mrs. Almeda, the only woman who has ever verbally
given me permission to protect myself, even if it meant
breaking bones.

To Mr. Craig, for speaking great wisdom, being a counsel,
friend and brother.

To Mrs. Bettina, who told me to write everything down.
Without that bit of information, this book
and connecting the dots would never have
happened.

To my family and my brother, whose love of
reading and writing caused me to catch up.
He is finally a great leader.
—DS

To my wife Sue.
Thanks and love.
—MS

Riding Shotgun

I am damaged.

So, I figured if I were going to tell a story, it was going to have to be told simply. I thought about putting the ending before the beginning so you'd at least have an idea about how things turn out, but a straight line is difficult enough for me. I'm going to tell this story the way it came out of my head.

The Law of the Jungle

Now this is the law of the jungle,
as old and as true as the sky:
And the wolf that shall keep it may prosper,
but the wolf that shall break it must die.
As the creeper that girdles the tree-trunk
the Law runneth forward and back —
For the strength of the pack is the wolf,
and the strength of the wolf is the pack
— Rudyard Kipling

Why I drive and the reasons for living

Some days, I need to drive. Some days, the rumble of the engine when I start it up is calming in its vibration. Some days, I want to drive with the windows down, my left arm getting a trucker's burn and the roar of the world swirling around in the cab. Some days, I drive with the windows up, running the cold air on my face in the summer and the warm air from the vents in the floor in winter.

In the night, the deep of the night, when the darkness is a friend and the small glowings of the dashboard show only sympathy for the machine, I like to drive. The white lines, the metaphor of the road, form the template of my journey, and I know it well. The routes and destinations change and the cargos vary from the interesting to the mundane.

My name is Paul David Wiley. I was called "Pauli" growing up, but David is my name of choice. I am a truck driver, for now. Not in the past and not for always. I am always a religious man, a man of God, an admirer of Jesus. Even so, I find it hard to figure out religion nowadays. Some people would call me a "Holy Roller," but at least I don't go around sporting a bow tie, accompanied by a friend dressed the same, knocking on doors with a pamphlet.

I don't mind the towel-heads, the Muslims, or the Jews with the beanies. I say that cheerfully and with no rancor. I mean, look at the Catholics if you want to call the fashion police. The men wear little slippers and brocaded satin outfits. Did Jesus tell them to dress that way? I don't think so. I just try and figure out what the words in the Book mean.

Speaking of books, I read a lot. It doesn't mean I understand everything. But the way I figure it, unless you leave a story behind, it's as if you haven't really existed.

So, here's my story, it's about predator and prey and how that relationship seems to exist most everywhere and is the most basic of principles. We are supposed to be at the top of the food chain. Seems that just means we're smart enough to eat each other and not think twice about it.

I work out of Superior, Wisconsin. This trip my destination was Edmonton, Alberta, Canada. I was carefully carrying a trailer full of Ashley furniture. I had gotten a late start and it was dusk before I left the city. Darkness filled the rearview mirror. Amber twilight edged the western horizon. The Peterbilt rode true.

More from David

I don't go back to Lawton often. As a kid, I played along the East Branch of Wolf Creek, not far from Cameron University, where my father worked. It was one of the good memories from my time in Lawton.

My mother Lilian died when I was ten. Her dying enraged my father even further. Ray looked good from the outside, a minor professor at a small, virtually unknown school, where he was known as fastidious. At home, he was feared. There were rules and you obeyed. His wife, my mother, obeyed and lived, black and blue and broken, until she gave up and died.

It's an old story—beaten, bullied and berated. As for me, by eighth grade, I could look him in the eye and take the beating. I took up wrestling in high school and waited.

One Sunday morning, we ran out of milk. I had the last of it on my corn flakes. He went into a tantrum, screaming, "You fucking horse. I pay for your food. I teach kids like you, fucking punks, and what do I have at home, a fucking lard ass of a kid, stupid."

When he reached to slap me, I pulled his arm toward me and threw him over my hip. I knelt on his back, twisted his arm and explained how things were going to be different. I whispered threats. He listened. I wrenched his arm until he screamed, then held it until he sobbed. I felt better. I finished my corn flakes.

I had a year left in high school. In that year, I became the predator, my father the prey. It had to be that way.

I would see him off to work with growls and quick movements. I tried to keep him off balance and afraid. I threatened him daily, reminded him of what he had done to my mother. I kept the one gun we had in the house, a Western Field 12-gauge shotgun, but carried two slugs in my pocket. Playing with them at the dinner table, I'd set the slugs up in front of my plate like two sentinels then, sometime during the meal, I'd say "Bang" and knock one over.

During my senior year in high school, I plotted. I was accepted at the University of Nebraska. On the day I left Lawton, I saw my father off to work, packed my things and loaded my truck. I did not look back and never saw my father again. I majored in business management and I was out in three and a half years. Numbers were my forte.

That last day, over and over again
Driving through the night

He thought of the four years he had spent doing a friend a favor. It had changed his life, no doubt about it. Lucy Santos had been Sgt. Santos in the Army. When he came back to the States from Iraq, he had looked her up. She was now running a group home for the State of Oklahoma in Tulsa. They met over beers at the Dustbowl Bar and Grill.

* * * * *

"Come over here, big guy," she said. "Give me a hand." That's not exactly what she said. She said, "David, I'm having trouble finding good people to work at the group home I head up. You've had some experience as an M.P. You have a college degree and look like an NFL tight end. I have to ask."

"My degree is in Business Management," I countered.

"The fact is, you have one," she replied. "You were able to finish. You have a work ethic, and that counts."

"Okay, how does being an M.P. translate into working on the staff at a group home? What do they say, 'Long periods of boredom punctuated by moments of terror?' I was trained to deal with men."

He stopped talking and peered at her.

Lucy Santos gave him a look, raised her eyebrow and waited. She knew silence was as important as words.

"Let me guess," he sighed. "These are big kids, some of them. Blacks, whites, Indians, Latino, a juvenile facility. Bad kids."

She nodded, "Yes, teenagers, a group home, though, not a jail; some of them do end up incarcerated. And yes, all colors, mostly poor. Ours is a level-four facility; there are five levels in the state. Kids at my place could still go either way."

She tugged at her earrings. "They're not bad kids; they're damaged. They've been beaten, bullied, and broken. That sounds like a bad song. These kids have been starved, locked up, tortured, punched out, raped, violated, and burned with cigarettes. Some have been left for dead. A few have tried to kill themselves. Sometimes they act like a pack of wolves. They need help, David."

They needed help. I needed help. How was this going to work?

"I have some issues, some anger issues." I looked away.

"We all do," she said, watching his face.

"I grew up in an abusive household," David said. "My dad beat my mother, broke her arm twice, and knocked out her front teeth. He beat me until I was big enough to beat him back. When I was little, I'd try to step in when he got to punching my mom around. He'd cuff me on the ears, slap my face backhanded."

"You understand," Lucy Santos replied. "If you understand, you can help. You're smart, but more than that, you have empathy. Plus, I understand you need a job."

* * * * *

That day, he had driven away from the home; the day he saw her standing in the rain had been his last day on the job. He had raced the Devil of Temptation to the finish line and won.

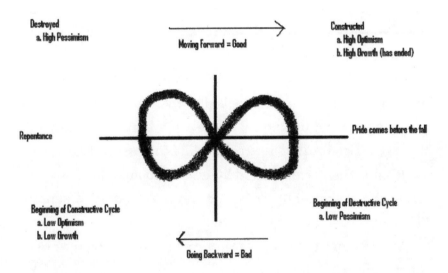

She...

S he was no wolf in sheep's clothing. Rebecca Wells was a wolf in wolf's clothing. Is there such a thing as a feline canine? Well, she was it and I knew I was in trouble when she waltzed into group with Mrs. Santos.

Staff would introduce a new client at the beginning of a group discussion session. Usually it was the boss who did the introducing, an authority figure who breaks the ice. In this case, it was Mrs. Santos. The classroom works as a place to observe reactions and by the end of group, everyone is used to the smell of each other.

She smelled vaguely of roses and, when she swung around to look at me, she looked at me. The young woman, and she was that at sixteen, had eyes of a clarity unusual at that age, disconcerting in a room full of furtive glances.

It's not often I call on God in the classroom. I don't want to waste the quarter, but I did that morning. I prayed simply, "Lord, protect me from temptation."

If I can mix religions, that prayer became a mantra over the months that followed.

Temptation. I think I heard God chuckling. I took long walks to avoid thinking about her. It just made it worse. I lifted weights, drove my pickup to the levee and fished with no bait.

Rebecca Wells speaks...

Men rape you and take your identity.

Men beat you and make you forget who you are.

Men bully you, steal your name.

No, no, no.
Not my father.
Not my priest.
Not the cop.

You can rape me, beat me and bully me, but you don't get to win. I do.

Speaking of me, my father said, "She's sick. I would never have done that to my own daughters. There are plenty of women here at work... I know women who would have..."

It happened. In the bedroom, bathroom, office, car, outside church.

She had slit her father's throat so many times (he had a smile below his chin), kicked him in the balls, broken his legs, gouged out his eyes. Finally, at age sixteen, she had looked him in the eye and told him she forgave him. "It's easy, you're such a pathetic bastard." But she couldn't save her mother, nor did she want to.

Rebecca Wells hailed from a crossroads named Hartshorne in the Jack Fork Mountains of southeast Oklahoma. A friend from grade school, Mina Carruthers, had moved to Tulsa with her family two years earlier but the girls had kept in touch. They were pen pals, actually wrote notes to each other. When she told Mina how things were at home, Mina replied with one word, "Come."

Rebecca was an athlete in an addictive, violent family. She took the blows and moved forward, looking for the unlocked door, the unlatched window.

She made it as far as Eutaula, where a McIntosh County deputy pulled in behind her as she walked along the gravel shoulder of the road. He got out of the squad car and stood with his right hand on the handle of his Glock.

She stood with her pack on her back, hip cocked. Then she blew a bubble quickly and popped it loudly in the silence between them. Afterward, she added squad car to the places she had been raped.

He dropped her at a grocery store where she was caught shoplifting steaks, had them down her jeans when the packaging broke, leaking blood onto her thigh. The letch who manned the security post was looking at her crotch when he noticed the bulge and blood. It was her ticket to the group home. At least now she got to eat, and the violence was less than the house in Hartshorne.

She fought to save herself. She had known who she was for as long as she could remember. Are some children born old? She was an adult from the womb. Her body spent years catching up to her mind.

Being awkward almost killed her. She knew better but her body wouldn't respond. She became gawky, then tall. "Rangy" was used to describe her. When she was sent to the home, she was five and a half feet tall and weighed one hundred pounds. She hadn't filled out yet but she knew it was coming. So did all of the boys and some of the girls.

You, my teacher, didn't take. You didn't even ask. I wanted you to ask, but I'm so glad you didn't.

I will remember you

"I will remember you, Mr. David," she thought. "I remember you trying not to look at me the first day. Every other face in the room, but not mine. It's as if you had to prepare to see me."

* * * * *

Now, in the rain, she saw him driving away. If he saw her, he didn't acknowledge it.

"I will remember you," she thought. "I remember watching your hands, hands that never touched me. I thank you for not touching me. If you had, there would be no future. Now the future is only unknown, not impossible.

"I hear you. I remember all the things you said that were never love. So many words describe you. You are the truth. Your words, wherever you found them, have kept me safe, given me hope, led me in the right direction, softened the blows of others, but never expressed love.

"Will the turning of a calendar page open the locks on the chest filled with the words of love? Will I always be damaged and way too young?"

She had been fighting to save herself for as long as she could remember. She knew her "self."

She was looking for a kindred spirit. That's wrong. She wasn't looking for anyone when she was shipped off to the group home.

Left behind and found again

I could have picked her up. I could have stopped my truck, opened the window and struck up a conversation. I could have waved, at least, or smiled. I did none of these.

My last morning had been grueling. Between the bullying, the threats of violence, the shouting, the crying, the urine in the hallway, and the crap on the bed, I was ready for a group home of my own. There was no humor this morning, no encouragement, no pats on a shoulder. It was stomach churning. I had been on the night shift and stayed to help when all hell broke loose.

I swear the kids had a group meeting. By the time I left around ten in the morning, it was raining and the wind was kicking up. I started up my truck and let the engine run. I eased the truck out of the lot and turned toward home.

She was standing behind a hedge about 100 feet from the bus stop, close enough to make a run for the bus, far enough away to skip notice. She was soaked and I could see her backpack sitting in a puddle. I didn't even slow down. I tried to make myself believe I hadn't seen her. But I had. She was from the home. I knew her. She lived in my dreams.

My conscience beat me up for an hour and a half before I went back to find her. She had disappeared. I went to the group home and asked if she had come back, only to find they hadn't missed her.

A search ensued. Calls to her mother went unanswered. My guess is the mother liked her gone and wouldn't lift a finger. The local cops were alerted but, my guess again, really didn't put much effort into the search. Another day, another kid gone.

That last day, over and over again.

But, my guess is again, no one really put much effort into the search. Another day, another kid gone.

I could have picked her up. It might have been trouble. Who am I kidding? Of course it would have been trouble. Putting an underage girl in my truck, even to give her a ride back to the home, was asking for it.

But now, five years later, I drive the roads and look at every young girl sitting, head down, at every truck stop. I slow for all the hitchhikers, though I don't pick them up. I glance in every booth at every truck stop.

The memory of her standing in the rain, or crying in her room, or laughing in the diner comes to me in the dark of the truck cab. I am alone and I wonder if she is as well.

The orca and the seal, the wolf
and the buffalo calf, Tom and Penny,
the small blond who works
at the gas station:
predator and prey, all of them ...

keep a notebook in my truck. It's in a carryall I keep on
the passenger seat of the cab, along with a spare pair of
jeans, an ASPCA t-shirt and my .357 Magnum. I wear a
Japanese survival knife on my belt. I keep a cooler with water,
candy bars, chips and sandwiches. The Peterbilt is home.
Driving is second nature to me now.

I'm just leaving International Falls and the border crossing
into Canada. I'm looking forward to a long night of driving
across the plains. The notebook keeps me company, I write
down phrases that strike me, sometimes only words. The
word for today is *carnal*. Relating to sensual desires and
appetites, earthly, temporal. I keep a dictionary in the truck,
too.

I guess I think of *carnal* as animal-like, base. In the Book of
Ecclesiastes, Solomon writes that God tests us so that we may
see that we are like animals. Will we not do to each other
exactly what the animals do to each other? Scientific studies
and analyses prove us right. Men are pigs and women are

whatever we call them. Where's the evidence for that way of thinking?

How in the world do we know whom to believe, the one with the louder voice or the one with better scientific data? Maybe the one with better connections? I'd choose the last one myself. Figure out whom to believe and live in the lap of luxury. Competition and faith go hand in hand. One man could be working to deceive for his own benefit and the other working to produce a righteous outcome. How can we know the difference?

Predators. Have you ever watched a television show and seen a predator in action? Whether it's a *Nova* story about lions on the Serengeti or a tale of sadism on *Criminal Minds*, predators are captivating. They are skilled in their execution, meticulous in sizing up the situation, deadly in the sureness.

Predators must size up the situation accurately. They must overcome the emotional attributes of the prey. Does the prey feel safe? Do they feel safe with the predator in their comfort zone? Can the predator overcome the physical attributes of the prey? What are the prey's strengths and weaknesses?

Once these questions are answered, victimization can proceed. The prey is captured. The animal gets to eat. We all watch on TV and think, "Wow, wasn't that gross?" Whether it's *Animal Kingdom*, *ABC Sports*, or murder and child abuse on the evening news, predators grab our attention.

We feel sorry for the prey, especially if it's a victim of human atrocity. Is the prey unaware of the predator, of the danger encroaching? We watch in fascination as the prey continues to swim, or feed. We think, "Why doesn't it do something?" We watch the show, oblivious to the fact of the predator closing in on us. It's all so exciting. When the hairs on the back of your neck stand up, turn around and look; it may be gaining on you.

Tonight I'm happy driving to the sounds of the truck. It is a song, and the whap of the wipers is comforting, as is the warm, wet smell of the earth in spring. I'd like to walk the furrows of a field of corn.

My mind wanders.

The five senses

I walked into the woods about four o'clock that day. It was dry. Walking toward the tree stand, the leaves crunched under my feet. There was no wind. I walked slowly. Once I had climbed up into the tree stand, the woods became quiet.

I used to hunt in a blind, some bushes I managed to hide behind, but a tree stand affords a better shot. It's basically a small chair and harness attached to a tree about 15 feet from the ground. From there, you shoot down at your prey. They don't even know you're there.

I sat motionless, doing my best to blend in with the trunk of the tree. There were no branches to hide me. I was hoping the deer wouldn't approach from the side, it would have revealed my profile and given my position away.

Time passed and I listened to the forest. What was that sound? Where did it come from? What animal made that noise? I slowly moved my head back and forth, left to right and back again. It was squirrels, running back and forth through the dry leaves.

Dusk approached and the forest came alive. Crunching noises surrounded me. Then I could see them—does, female deer, moving around everywhere. It was a few weeks before the rut but the deer were moving. What was moving them? I watched as three does moved quickly through a cornfield, but they didn't offer a shot. I kept watching.

Then two small-spike bucks flew by, their eight-inch antlers showing how young they were. I was new to deer hunting at the time and would have taken a shot at one of them, but no shot presented itself. I continued sitting quietly. Then *he* appeared. The smaller males were being moved by a dominant buck, a brute, a monarch of the forest, massive and big-bodied.

I saw his antlers first. He was promenading up a ridge and his antlers gave him away. He had no idea I was in the woods, no idea. He walked with all the confidence of a king. He walked comfortably along the ridge and stopped to browse. My breath was too large for my chest and I started shaking. Buck fever.

It was my time. I put an arrow through him, a thirty-yard, double-lung shot. He charged ten yards and dropped.

To this day, I don't think that deer ever knew what hit him. He did not pick up the hunter in the tree. He did not realize I was out there. When I saw him go down, I knew I had killed a "wall- hanger."

Quietly, I gathered my gear, climbed down from the deer stand and got safely to the ground. When I approached him, I realized he was big, bigger than anything I had ever shot before. I tried dragging him to the trail but he weighed too much. It took three of us to drag him out of the woods and he ended up field- dressed at 242 pounds. He was a giant ten-pointer.

* * * * *

Predator and prey. I learned from the deer and transferred those lessons to the group home. It takes me
back. Did I mention I worked for a group home in Tulsa,
Oklahoma, for four years? I did, didn't I?

The lessons are simple. Executing them is another matter. I
visit the group home every day. Voices in the dead of night
take me back. The smell of bleach and urine. A child huddled
under a bridge. Young panhandlers. All take me back.

Snap.

Emotional Displacement in Psychological Cycles

Character issues with Donny Garcia

Some things are the same for teachers everywhere. There's a blackboard (or whiteboard or green board), chalk, markers, and a desk and chair.

The kids filed in and took their places. A few were sullen, a few smiled, and a few were barely able to keep their anger from bubbling over. It was a typical Monday in the neighborhood. Mr. Rogers wasn't in the building, I was.

Donny Garcia. Just between you and me, the dumb little shit never apologizes for his behavior, doesn't ask for forgiveness and, because of low trust choices, bursts out verbally and physically instead of being patient and waiting. He wants to control the situation, manipulating by having a story and sticking to it, instead of admitting he was wrong or lying. He practices deception but isn't very good at it. I'm just trying to get him to stay within the boundaries, rules and limitations of the middle boys.

Donny Garcia

Name: Donny Garcia

Affect	Mood	Participation	Behavior
Positive	Stable	Cooperative	Compliant

D onny Garcia had been in the home a month when I had my first encounter with the boy. He was thirteen at the time. All he could look at were crotches, either sex. He was jealous of one and curious about the other. All he could think of was acne.

One evening, while sweeping, I noticed Donny hanging down at the end of the hallway with the older boys. They were gathered around him for some reason; it looked as though he was telling a story. Finally one of the older boys patted him on the shoulder. He continued for some time longer than I thought reasonable. It seemed to me he was doing this to push his limits and wanted to see how long he was allowed to stay with the older boys.

As I approached the group, the older boys gave half-salutes or touched their foreheads.

"Evening, Mr. Dave," said one on behalf of the group.

"Evening boys," I replied. "Young Mr. Garcia, I'd like a word with you."

Donny did what amounted to a little dance for the older boys and said, "Shit, Mr. Dave, I got to talk with the guys here. Come back later."

And you know what? That little snot gave me a shit-eating grin to go with it. I could have bopped him on the spot. But I had been trained and had a degree. I gave him the glare, all two hundred and forty pounds of it.

Okay, truth be told, I gave him about a hundred pounds of look. He was a little kid and I wanted some in reserve. It was enough. The boy followed directions and went to his room.

The following Sunday, Donny poked his head into my office and started running off at the mouth, "Mr. Dave, you have got to let me do some stuff. I gotta have some choices here. Those ankle biters get to pick out their own socks. When do I get to do that? I'm thirteen, for Christ's sake. I can pick my nose, I can pick my own socks."

"Next time, knock," I said quietly.

He made his way into the office, warily.

He kept on talking, "And I can iron. We got to iron our clothes. I can do that, I know how to do that. I did that at home."

"You hit your sister with an iron, a hot iron," I replied. "No iron for you. Donny, everyone here earns privileges, earns their freedom in small steps, small responsible steps."

"You a asshole warden, Mr. Dave the fuck." He put his hands on his hips.

I spent a long time looking at him. Finally, he fidgeted. "Go to your room until you cool down. Another staff member will be down soon. This is not a good way to start your Sunday, Donny. Let's see if we can start over."

He let a wad of air out and turned away. "You got to let me have some room. The kids are picking on me, Mr. Dave." He calmly shut the door and I could hear his footsteps down the hall.

He cooled down and I went and sat with him later. I got tough and told him he could pick out his socks and his damn underwear, too, if he would watch his mouth.

Mother made me wash my mouth out with soap. Ivory soap.

Sometimes my visits to the group home don't amount to more than a glare in the window. Sometimes the smell of the restaurant at a truck stop sets me off. Sometimes it's the clatter of a dishwasher, a door slamming, crying or kids acting out and parents giving up and slapping them in public.

Now, instead of taking it home with me, I step in when I see a child's feet off the ground, a mother or father yanking on an arm, wrist already splotched with black and blue. I step in now and take my chances. We must step in, step up, for the children. Take on a bully. We all know one.

Sunday at the Home

One weekend, Donny Garcia asked me for a thumbtack. "I want to hang a poster," is what he said.

"Yes," I said, not thinking it would be a big deal. But I couldn't find one. When I attended our monthly meeting, on the first Wednesday of each month, I found out the kids were trying to pierce their ears with thumbtacks, and that was why Donny was asking for one.

But the kid was adamant, even when confronted by the staff. "I got a poster and all I want to do is put it on my wall, Mr. David."

When I asked him what poster, he didn't have an answer. I think the kid was going to stick to that story, whether he got his ear pierced or not, but the motive for the thumbtack was to pierce his ear.

It was normal for him to push the issue, peer pressure, but the reason he gave me was part of a manipulative story to get me to say yes. The situation played out over a week.

There had to be more to it, for he became increasingly abusive as the week wore on, both to me and the rest of the staff.

On Sunday, I was cleaning up after an eight-year-old boy named Bobby Martin. He had had an accident and peed his pants while waiting in the hallway.

Donny happened on the two of us. "Why don't you make him lick it up, Mr. Dave. That boy ain't going to make it to ten. He got to be taught a lesson. Let me give him a kick for you."

He spit on the carpet and gave me a look, "Mr. Upchuck and the little pisser."

It was timeout for Donny.

"Go to your room and wait for me. Consider your behavior and what you can do to improve it. And you are going to dine in your room, buddy."

He turned and screamed, "You asshole! You nothin' but a prick. I'm gonna take care of you one day. You are on my list."

I yelled back, "To your room, Garcia."

I watched him kick the wall and growl at Bobby as he flung himself into his room. I listened as he punched the wall, over and over again. Finally it grew quiet. I cleaned up after Bobby, helped him change into clean pants and took him to the diner.

Then I went to Donny's room to see if he had calmed down. He hadn't. The boy waited until he had my attention and proceeded to punch the wall again, this time while screaming at the top of his lungs, "Fuck this place! Fuck this place!" He then walked past me and out the back of the building.

I didn't know if he was going AWOL or to the diner. When I stepped out the side door, I saw him walking past the staff car and watched as Mr. Devlin confronted Donny.

The boy never had much sense and took a swing at Devlin while continuing to yell, "Fuck you, fuck all of you."

Nothing Devlin or I could say or do calmed the boy down. We had to put him in a Crises Prevention Intervention (CPI) hold that lasted three minutes. This allowed him a chance to calm down, regroup, and begin cooperating. We walked him back to his room and I let him sit for fifteen minutes before talking with him.

"Are you okay?" I asked him. "Are you ready to try the diner?"

The boy nodded, "Yes."

Sometimes a treatment plan ends up being simple. Donny's treatment plan involved a struggle for existence and he is doing a lot better than when he first arrived. Staff protection has helped him develop into a better human being. He is going to be able to understand his social needs and will eventually leave healthier. He has gained some self-respect and is starting to plan a future for himself. He plans on joining the Army.

In the support group, we talked about isolation and independence. If we are isolated, then we have not built a proper support group to help us live independently.

At another session, we discussed primary motives and the reasons individuals might pursue a goal or dream. What pushes someone to continue going forward even when there are trials in life? Donny's motives revolve around family and learning to be more competent at certain things in life.

As part of the treatment plan, we watched *Lord of the Flies,* identified the maturity level of the kids portrayed in the film and the corresponding outcome for each kid. We defined maturity and talked about how we are meant to mature over time. The importance of mentors was brought up in relation to the movie. The boys had no mentors. The boy who became the leader in the movie was not a mentor but a predator. When the kids started killing each other, it became evident the wrong leader was in place. There are dire consequences to losing one's morality.

If the boys in the group home were a wolf pack, Donny would be a pack member, not an alpha male.

Snap.

Another kid, another episode

Phillip Lovell is struggling for basic survival. The staff has kept him safe and teachers have helped him learn. There are solutions, but sacrifices have to be made and values instilled. He needs role models. He feels his attitudes and perceptions are better. The boy's motivation is money. And we say he's not normal.

Phillip Lovell

Name: Phillip Lovell

Affect	Mood	Participation	Behavior
Positive	Stable	Cooperative	Compliant

While cleaning rooms in the morning, another staff member, Mr. Craig, asked Phillip Lovell to clean his room. A short time later, when I went to inspect Phillip's room, he had towels on the bathroom floor, pencils on the ground, and trash stuffed into his chest of drawers. I asked him to clean up his room and take care of these items.

After giving him some time, I went back and confronted him. He said, "Mr. Craig is fine with my room. Deal with it."

Nothing had been taken care of.

"Get up off your bed and clean this room."

He gave me the finger with a waist-high gesture and said, "You get paid to clean this shit up."

It had been a weekend of shit with this mouthy teenager. "Time to close your mouth," I spat.

He balled up his fist and yelled. I grabbed one of the drawers from the chest and dumped it out on the floor. There was nothing but trash in it. I dumped a second drawer on the carpet, more trash and pissy clothes. The stench was horrible. I knew I was becoming upset and gave myself a time-out, walking up the hallway to collect my thoughts.

When I returned a few minutes later, I saw Tremaine Washington and Chuck Stratton talking with Phillip outside the door to his room. I couldn't hear what was said. Finally Phillip spotted me, walked up to me and said quietly to my face, "I can take you."

I walked away to find more staff and apprised them of the situation. We called in Tremaine and gave him a chance to come clean. He chose a bad route and stayed silent.

I went back to Philip's room to see if he had made any progress. He was sitting on his bed. I brought Mr. Craig into the room. He said simply, "Clean up your room, Phillip."

Phillip balled up his fists, gave a shout and launched himself at Mr. Craig. I joined Mr. Craig in the fracas and we applied a CPI hold. The boy continued to fight and kick. We got him under control and he was able, finally, to understand what needed to be taken care of.

After processing, he got his room squared away and accepted his responsibility, saying he knew his room should have been cleaned up a long time ago.

Phillip runs in the middle of the pack but watch out, this animal bites when you're not looking.

Snap.

Words...

The forms used by the Oklahoma Community Programs were a minefield. Step on a word and break your mother's back. Sticks and stones can break your bones, but words can never hurt you. The pen is mightier than the sword.

Affect:

Apathetic—Without emotion or interest. Detached. Lethargic.

Worried—To cause anxious uneasiness in. Concern.

Positive—Of a constructive nature. Affirmative. Upbeat.

Passive—Submitting without objection or resistance. Resigned.

Bright—Full of promise. Mentally quick or original.

Hyper—Exaggerated energy.

Seductive—Tending to seduce. Alluring. Bewitching.

Impulsive—Characterized by unthinking boldness. Brash. Foolhardy.

Mood:

Silly—Displaying a lack of forethought, good taste.

Agitated—In a state of anxiety or uneasiness.

Stable—Not easily moved or shaken, firm, secure.

Sad—In low spirits, blue, dejected, depressed.

Anxious—Agitated, concerned, distressed.

Irritable—Having or showing a bad temper cranky.

Hostile—Belligerent, combative, militant.

Labile—Forgetful, wandering.

Angry—Feeling or showing anger, mad.

Participation:

Cooperative—Willingness to cooperate.

Passive—Accepting without resistance or objection.

Evasive—Intentionally ambiguous or vague.

Avoidant—To keep away from.

Uncooperative—Not willing to cooperate

Behavior:

Dependent—Contingent on something or someone else.

Compliant—Inclined or disposed to comply.

Oppositional—The act of opposing or being in conflict.

Demanding—Requiring constant effort or attention.

Manipulative—To manage or influence shrewdly.

The words followed the clients; that's what we called the inmates, the children, the kids, the students. When I filled out the forms each day, I thought of the future. Some were hyper, hostile, evasive and demanding. Others were worried, silly, passive and dependent. But to send those labels into the future with the kids was to flag them for the rest of their lives. I was looking, as we all were, for bright, stable, cooperative and compliant young people. What have we done? Where are they now?

That dash and all it means

When you think of it, sometimes the letters are just as scary as the words. As in IED, improvised explosive device, a simple bomb. And the little things of grammar are scary as well, like the dash. As in bi-polar, and post-traumatic stress disorder.

Bi-polar can be characterized by both manic and depressive episodes. The manic and depressive phases may last for weeks or months. It can't be cured but treatment may help. So says my therapist.

Post-traumatic stress disorder is a mental health condition that's triggered by a terrifying event, either experiencing it or witnessing it. Symptoms may include flashbacks, nightmares and extreme anxiety as well as uncontrollable thoughts about the event. I often visit the group home in nightmares and flashbacks. Smells and sounds set me off. Brown carpeting keeps me anxious. So says my therapist.

ADHD, attention deficit hyperactivity disorder, is a medical condition that affects how well someone can sit still, focus and pay attention. People with ADHD have differences in the parts of their brains that control attention and activity. That means they may have trouble focusing on some tasks and subjects. So says my therapist.

I live with conditions and am visited by episodes. I'm told these letters apply to me, but it seems it depends on who I talk to, clergymen, therapists, teachers, cops or friends. I know I'm damaged somehow, but that doesn't mean I can't be a good, functional human being.

I managed to get a degree in business administration. Talk about bi-polar, right and left brain, I think my brain works on the front-back principle. And there's that dash again.

Give me numbers, lots of numbers, as I cross the prairies dark and dim. Schedule me and leave it on the clipboard.

I like maps, though I use GPS to locate addresses I don't know. There's something about spreading a map across the table in a booth at the I-Hop in Grand Island, Nebraska. I've got maps in the truck. You could trace my travels by the stains: chili sauce from Albuquerque, barbecue sauce from a basket of wings in Roanoke, runny eggs from an order of biscuits and gravy, sunny-side-up on top from the Breakwater Café in Ironwood in the Upper Peninsula of Michigan.

Maps. It was called orienteering in the Scouts. It was the same in the service. I have a ball compass I salvaged from a 53 Desoto. It floats and swings, pointing the way for the Peter-bilt. I ride along, listening to the Native American station as I cut across North Dakota.

Snap.

* * * * *

It's almost electrical. One moment I'm driving, drinking coffee out of the Thermos, watching the prairie go by and snap, I'm walking down the hallway at the group home.

Snap.

* * * * *

Electrical. I can almost smell the ozone. I don't always go back to the group home. Sometimes, I end up in the tree stand, watching and waiting.

Snap.

* * * * *

Sometimes the snap means a visit to Iraq, fear contained and pushed into a salute. "Hey, big guy, come over here and volunteer." So says the sergeant in my dreams.

Snap.

Looking in the mirror

We are all, even the richest and most powerful, prey at least once in our life. Once set in motion, the grim reaper's scythe is forever.

I am six feet two inches tall and weigh two hundred and forty pounds. Size often denotes a predator and I admit I dress to size, jeans and steel-toed work boots. Carhartt is my clothier and Caterpillar my haberdasher. I wear shades and sport a buzz cut.

I was in the Army, even got away with an honorable discharge. My VA therapist is in Iron Mountain, Michigan. I drive from Superior because I can talk to her. She appreciates my situation.

So, somebody is worried about predators on the prowl and sees me walking towards them, they cross the street. In the middle of the block. In traffic.

Standing still, I intimidate. Little guys don't like me. On the other hand, even when I was little, I was big. "David, could you mow the lawn? David, could you get the heavy boxes down from the attic? David, come here, I need a big guy."

I remember the sergeant in Iraq. He said, "David, I need a couple of big guys to volunteer for a mission. You and the Ski." He meant Lapinski, the other big guy.

Even so, looming large has usually been a good thing. Size does mean power. It also makes you a target. Taking down a little guy doesn't mean shit to a tree. Now, you take down a big guy, think David and Goliath, you are a hero for the ages. Samson and Delilah, there's another story. Feminine wiles take the place of a sling and stone.

A black t-shirt and a leather jacket saves me a lot of talking. Work gloves stuck out of a back pocket and a Leatherman on my belt completes the regalia.

I wear shades. The key to a predator-prey relationship is in the eyes. Day or night, darkness or light, it is in the eyes. Goodness, cunning, fear, power: all in the eyes. Who is hunting whom?

The eyes and whispers. I heard things, listened to the boys and girls pimp each other in the diner, disrespect each other in the hallways and threaten each other in the shadows.

* * * * *

If you live in northern Wisconsin like I do, chances are your doctor will hail from India or Pakistan. Dr. Singh tapped my knee with his rubber hammer. It was the only diagnostic tool I recognized. I take that back. I know what an X-ray is. I was having some trouble with my left knee. I had a hunch there was some shrapnel from the IED that rolled our Humvee in Iraq. We were thrown over rather than rolled. Big explosion.

When I came to, everything hurt. My knee was bloody, every joint ached, my goggles were cracked. Hell, my helmet was cracked. I knew for sure it was Wednesday and told the medic. He wanted me to focus on his fingers and told me it was Friday.

My head felt stuffed with cotton. I couldn't hear clearly. I kept trying to blink away the encroaching gray but fell over onto my side and threw up instead. Off we went to Ramstadt, Germany. Speak German? *Nein, Fraulein.*

It was years ago. Whatever war that was, it's over now, mostly. Sort of. And we are left with the unintended consequences. Iraq wasn't too bad, only five thousand or so dead Americans. We can save many wounded soldiers now, give them new arms, plates in their heads, springs for legs.

Now we can use a 3-D printer and fashion new hands, set the wounded up with cameras for eyes. Can't do that? Well, then, how about a wheelchair complete with a computer activated by a veteran's breath, all that's left that is his to control.

I'm not right and I'm pissed. I'm listening to this little mahogany man with a name I can't pronounce tell me, "You should have disability, soldier." He pronounced it "sojer."

"You collect VA," he added. "Go fishing, hunt trophies." He sounded like the owner of the local BP. The rhythms of Delhi right here in Superior, Wisconsin.

I snapped, "You keep talking in that pansy-ass way of yours, Doc, and I will kill you for your lilt." My therapist told me later lashing out is a sign of latent schizophrenia. The threats are part of the disease, not really meant.

Needless to say, he was the last civilian doctor I went to. The same type of episode happened at the VA in Iron Mountain and the Army doctor looked at me and laughed. She said, "You're the third non-com today that threatened me. I'll remind you I'm a captain. So, stand up, salute and haul your ass off to your therapist. She'll likely smack you down as well, soldier." She didn't say "sojer."

My therapist told me to stop cleaning my guns at the kitchen table. "It gives you ideas," she said and looked me in the eye. "When you become military, you leave all the others outside. Your family wears eye patches, has had plastic surgery, bone grafts, have been fitted for prosthetics. Welcome home, soldier."

My therapist knows I have a girlfriend. I haven't mentioned how we first met, at the group home where she was a client and I was on the staff. I haven't told my therapist.

She was sixteen when I first met her, a long shank of a girl. She was tall with sharp angles, a winning smile and a ferocious mind. She would come at you with eyes and words, boring in with both, a magnificent animal. But she had been raped and beaten as a kid. She came out of that home with her teeth bared and her hair on end.

I had been working at the home for three years when she showed up. What is a working morality? How do you make the day to day decisions involved? I mean, she was a good- looking girl. More than that, she was attractive in a visceral way. I knew she was trouble. I watched, then saw her watching me as well.

A letter

David's search for Rebecca was more analog than digital. His was more of a classic quest. There were days he dressed her in long gowns. But he was a realist as well, pragmatic anyway, and it became second nature to check the booths at truck stops, watch the curb sitters at the gas stations and look for upturned faces at the freeway on-ramps. More than that, he made a habit of going on-line, where he Googled her name and checked the police blotters in the newspapers.

He filled one notebook, then another. One of his demons, one that rode with him in the cab of the truck, was depression, which brought sadness and remorse. Therapists are few on the road, so David wrote letters. He was having a tire repaired at an intersection known as Last Chance, Colorado. He felt the name said it all. David wrote the young woman he had left behind:

> *Dear ... ,*
>
> *Time goes on and I have grown older. I'm writing this in hopes you will continue to pursue your dreams and goals in life. I would like to share with you some of the things I have learned about humanity, being human amid the constant bombardment of negative information and behavior. The future looks grim.*

I have been reading books. I want to comprehend that which surrounds us. They say man was created in God's image and woman was created for beauty. That's not word for word, but is a close generalization. If what they write is true, then this formula might be true as well:

Humans – God = animals.

I've read Ecclesiastes. It mentions that one day we will all figure out that our life cycles are very much like those of the animals. Freud studied us like animals without a God. And so we are. This should be cause for alarm. The baby boomers, the biggest generation of all, is getting older, about to retire and must give themselves to caretakers of a younger generation that might not give a shit. As a society, we have become animalistic instead of humanistic. We should be working toward caring, loving, and being more Christ-like.

Even the churches stoop to new levels. I do not feel comfortable in many churches, the First Baptist, for instance. Too many predators trying to victimize followers. I need forgiveness, too. That forgiveness is the beauty of the Gospels, the beauty of the reconciliation ministry of Christ that Paul writes about in the New Testament. For some reason, when I get active in a church, I do not see this working. I actually see the opposite, a predator versus prey relationship and hostility towards God, instead of forgiveness and love towards mankind.

Our society is being held back by fears, anxiety and every mental health issue known to the psychologists. Freud. How is it that we believe Freud can help people when he couldn't help himself? Christ can heal the mind, the psychology and the human as a whole, as long as we use the Word of God for people instead of against them.

Predators (preachers, pastors and priests) cripple the same brothers and sisters in Christ they are supposed to be blessing. Instead they are made fun of, talked about behind their backs, cursed and isolated and all for what? So we'll think higher of you?

The truth of reconciliation has been stolen. I might steal it back, but I am not a thief, I am a producer. I forgive them. I'd like to do this face to face, but I can't. They will use the Word against me, as a lever, instead of for me. I have a place in the kingdom as a co-heir, a brother, accepted even with my faults.

Using the Word of God for people instead of against them is one of the most compassionate and loving things we can do for a person. The Word of God allows your heart to help cast down arguments of darkness in high places. The Word of God helps heal a person's view of themselves. The Word of God allows understanding of our fears and anxieties. Experience teaches us we must make moves to become the person God intended us to be.

We must build boundaries, protect and take care of those we love. As individuals and as a country we must reclaim our leadership. We must be the head and not the tail.

The mechanic rapped on the door of the truck. It was time to get back on the road.

The Law of the Jungle, continued...

Cub-right is the right of the yearling.
From all of his pack he may claim
Full-gorge when the killer has eaten;
and none may refuse him the same.

Suicide at the Diner

Y ou don't swing a lot of weight when you're eight years old and stuck in a group home. When you're under-sized, pee in your pants when an older boy looks at you and still suck your thumb, you are in dire straits, a prey looking for teeth to come gnashing.

Bobby Martin

Name: Bobby Martin

Affect	Mood	Participation	Behavior
PASSIVE	EVASIVE	COOPERATIVE	COMPLIANT

I 'm back at the desk in the front of the room. Bobby Martin didn't show up for breakfast. I went to his room to have a talk and found him curled up on his bed. "Bobby, what is going on with you?"

"I don't know," He said, not looking up. "I'm a crypt killer. I am a crypt killer."

"Okay," I replied, "I know you're a crypt killer. I hope we don't get a Crypt gang member in the hallway. Have a seat on your dresser. Let's talk this out."

He cried and said, "I'm sick of this place. I'm going to kill myself. I'm going to stab myself in the diner."

"Okay, prove it." I replied. I waited while he thought about it. "Bobby, I'm trying to help you. What is going on? Just be honest with me, tell me what you would want everybody to do if you could."

"I need to be back on my medication," he said, "There are a lot of medications in this land. I need some of them."

"Bobby," I said, "I believe you should be back in diapers. You can't seem to handle your bowels. Are you okay if I write something up and refer you to Mrs. Santos about this?"

"Yes," he said softly.

He curled up again. I threw a blanket over him and left him in his room. I think the boy would like to improve, but can't because he's hopeless. Whatever he chooses isn't right, so why care. Bobby believes no one can solve his problems. The older he gets, the more he will look to suicide. Sooner or later, he will be successful. He is in a Catch-22 situation where there are no good outcomes, therefore, he is powerless, emasculated. I did ask him if he forgave his uncle.

"No," he replied. "No."

Since Bobby got to the home, there has been a noticeable decrease in his ability to handle his bowel movements. The boy must be asked many times before he will do the task assigned to him. Staff members are frustrated. Bobby's hygiene has gone downhill since he stopped wearing diapers. The hallway smells like shit, to put it bluntly.

Either Bobby is failing our program or we are failing Bobby. When I questioned Bobby, I realized he has a major sense of hopelessness. It doesn't allow him to see things clearly.

He's only a boy. Why would a boy cover himself in his own feces? It was a long time before the answer dawned on me. I don't think I wanted to believe my conclusion. He figured the shit was protection, a last-ditch defense against an uncle who was a predator. Fear is the boy's constant companion.

When I ask Bobby to get ready in the morning, he puts off doing anything until everyone is frustrated and upset with him. I would attempt to redirect or correct his behavior and he would often jump on his bed facing down, much like a dog groveling. He has a lot more fear in his heart than we realize. When I pick him up, stand him up, he will usually cry, then he gets dressed and follows directions. His fear holds him back from experiencing a normal life.

He is frustrated and confused because nothing he does is ever right. We need to move this child from a life of hopelessness and fear to one of hope and victory. How do we do this? And his grades. He is failing in everything except poetry.

He hasn't forgiven his uncle for what he did. I wouldn't either. However, even I have had to learn to forgive my enemies. He must learn to do the same. Failure to forgive means continued hopelessness, bitterness and confusion. He must be empowered to protect himself from his uncle. If he does not forgive his uncle, he will continue to be victimized. Victory through forgiveness.

Bobby has been hiding his bowel movements in his room. His room reeks. The hallway reeks. I learned he is afraid how the staff will respond to his problems. I think this fear is costing him his recovery, if there is such a thing for this kid. Other staff members think he is lazy and just doesn't want to change. He gets the urge to take a crap, and instead of choosing to go to the restroom, he will just go in the corner.

I'm trying to be the boy's advocate. What if there is something wrong medically? What if his nerves are damaged and he can't feel anything because of the sexual abuse? I have no idea what abuse can do to a little male child. I know that can cause irreparable damage to the reproductive organs of a small female child. There seems to be no hope for the future. Maybe he should care because we do. We need to capitalize on Bobby's ability to rebound.

Group sessions were sometimes beyond Bobby's understanding. We talked about teachers and the security a teacher provides. Bobby participated as best he could. He knows enough to treat a teacher with respect.

I talked with Bobby about the emotions he was having on the inside versus the emotions he was showing people. It was a little beyond the kid. So was the session on self-control.

If this bunch of boys was a wolf pack, Bobby would be one of the last at the carcass, and the rest of the wolves would be nipping at him for that.

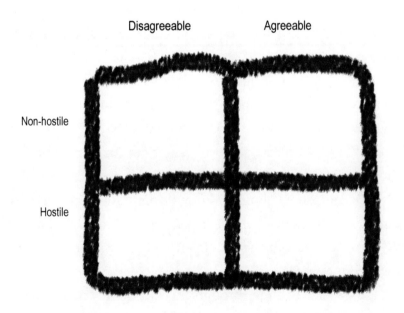

Mrs. Santos' new door

Lucy Santos had black hair going gray, worn in a bun. She sported tats on both arms, the left one a cross with flowers, the right an eagle with lightning bolts. She swung her Mexican weight around, but she was a good administrator, delegated authority and watched your back. I had been in a firefight with her and trusted her instincts. And she cared.

"I have a door on my office. A door is a simple thing, marking territory, controlling entrances and exits. Look closely at the next ten doors you come across, metal, wood, plastic.

"The door to my office was replaced last week. I worried about my old wood door, two panels of thin plywood. The knob was loose and the lock didn't work. Now I have a metal door that looks like wood. My new door has a peephole and the lock works from a buzzer at my desk.

"My old door? Rage splinters doors. Rage in a five-foot-ten-inch, 180-pound, 16-year-old mixed race (Indian and White) boy is physical, violent, roaring loud, crashing, focused mayhem.

"That's what came through my old door. I'm still here. It was a call for help, though. And it's my job to listen."

I went back to the staff room and unlocked the door. The staff room door was kept locked on general principles. The kids didn't need to know more than they did about the staff. Like wild dogs, they searched for any opening, any weakness.

In his book, *The Promise*, author Robert Crais says this about predators, "The African lion makes a kill only twice out of every ten hunts. Leopards do better, catching their prey twenty-five percent of the time, and cheetahs do best of all the big cats, with a kill ratio of nearly fifty percent. The deadliest four-legged African predator is not a big cat. It cannot be outrun or outdistanced, its pursuit is relentless, and it captures its prey nine out of every ten hunts. The most dangerous predator in Africa is the wild dog."

Someone knocked twice on the staff room door. I waited but it wasn't repeated. Doors gave you time to prepare, a chance to decide. Open it? Wait? Find another exit? A rap on the door can cause panic, but no door is worse. A locked door assures some safety. For a child in a group home, a locked door with a staff member in a chair outside means sleep. There are dreams we all dream but nightmares do not slip unseen into the room. Trust means regular breathing, sometimes snoring. Nice sounds in a room at night.

I thought a door with a peephole was a good idea until I read a mystery where someone was stabbed in the eye with an ice pick. Through the peephole. Now I stand to one side of the door or the other and ask who's there.

A door wasn't mentioned in Maslow's hierarchy of needs. A door, or the idea of a door, ranks just above air, water, food, clothing and shelter from the elements. Physical safety may rank as number one for victims of abuse. There is no healing, no mending without safety, without shelter from violence.

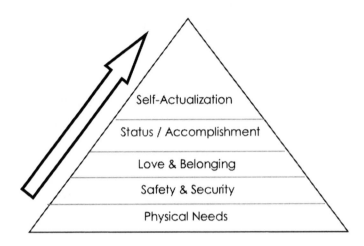

I had five minutes before group. Part of any day for staff members was going over the reports clipped to the bulletin board. Usually short and concise, they detailed lesson plans that worked and kids who didn't. Outbursts were listed, as were good sessions and shining moments. There were always surprises.

The group session reports were glanced at for certain words that served as flags. Portions were marked in pink, yellow, green and blue. Needed information was passed verbally among the staff. No paper trails with justifications, just hunches, guesses, instinct, feelings, vibes, looks, whispers and bumps in the night. Watch for this one, that one, those two.

Courage my young friends, courage

hen we show courage, we can effect change. With courage, kids at the group home do better at school, at the home and in society in general. Joseph Black is a sad young man who alternates between being compliant and demanding.

Joseph Black

Name: Joseph Black

Affect	Mood	Participation	Behavior
Worried	Sad	Cooperative	Compliant

ala-Land is a destination booked often on Group Home airways. You can check in, but it is hard to check out. Joseph Black's courage is tinged with sadness. He wears a cloak of inevitability. He thinks the future is predetermined. Sad at thirteen, Joseph doesn't just hang a long face, he is truly sad, bone tired sad. All he has known is hurt and abuse. His father's slaps grew into punches. His father called him a wuss, prissy, a little faggot.

As Joseph got older the words matured and he was bitch slapped and buggered. Is that a European word?

He was sent to the group home on the same day his mother went into the emergency room to have her broken jaw wired shut. It was a good day, all in all, his father went to jail. The kid had hopes, but when he was introduced at a group session an older boy whistled. The hopes died.

In the pack, Joseph worries at the edges, looking for dropped morsels, stealing when a back is turned.

Trucking...

started out running a KW (Kenworth). It had a 300 Cummins motor and a 4x4. Most argue that it is a sixteen-speed, but not true. It was similar in theory to the "triplex," but the 3x5 did in fact have 15 "speeds" to go along with the fifteen gears. The 4x4 had twin sticks and sixteen combinations (gears), but only thirteen different speeds.

There are four different gears in the first series on the main transmission. After that you only use the last three of the four possibilities (the first auxiliary gear of the last three gears on the main was actually the very same gear as the fourth gear in the series preceding on the main and was only used in the event of an upgrade or a headwind). Still, you could get shot trying to tell some dimwit that his 4x4 was just a thirteen-speed. Math is hard.

I ran "her" hard. I always told her I'd never like her as long as I had her, but we developed a bond. I say "her" just in reference, but there was actually a very masculine personality to my truck, and I did think of it as one of the guys. There was a time, and I'm being totally honest, that I was in a Master's Inn motel in the Carolinas, and I noticed that...standing in front of the NFL playoff game on my television set, and then looking out the window at my truck...the truck would not see the TV through the window.

I had no strong perception that the truck gave a damn about the NFL even though it was the playoffs… but with no huge effort on my part…I went out and jockeyed that truck to where it could see, unobstructed, the TV and the game. I had no thought stronger than I'd like someone to do the same for me…and I left the curtain open.

In January of last year, I got the Pete … the Peterbilt. It is a twin screw (tandem-drive axle) like the KW, but my first "conventional." My other tractors had been COEs, cab-over-engine, but this was a throwback to the 1940's timeless style of long hoods and tall stacks.

The peripheral players see an old-fashioned machine of dubious style, the hard-core drivers and the "wannabees" see familiarity, utility and timeless class. This is the Cadillac of the trucking world—powerful, quiet and clean. It's by far the most genteel of my trucks, and yet covers the ground with such effortless dominance that I call her "The Beast."

* * * * *

The black Peterbilt sat idling on the gravel edge of the terminal. I sat in a window booth of the restaurant, finishing the last of a two burger breakfast. There's something about hamburgers for breakfast. I peeled off a twenty for the meal, two tuna sandwiches and a refilled Thermos. There was enough room in the twenty for a three dollar tip.

Outside, the air was fresh and smelled like newly mown hay. The fresh-cut fields surrounding the truck stop accounted for that. I walked to the cab of the truck, admired the gloss of the new paint job, and rubbed my hand over the lightning bolts painted on the door. I eased the truck out of the line and made my way to the freeway entrance. Getting back on the road was always a relief. My own demons rode with me, but were quiet and arranged themselves around the cab. I was never long in one place and always leaving. It suited me. I poured a cup of coffee from the thermos and put it in the cup holder. I turned north.

Though I'm always on a schedule, I leave time to drive the back roads. I like the old state highways and often make better time than taking the freeways. And I get to see the towns the way the residents see them, not from the bypass. I like to ride the trains for the same reason, you get to see the backyards, the washing hanging from the lines, collections of plastic toys, dogs who live their lives at the end of a chain. Backyards are private moments.

Driving the old highways gives me a chance to look for her. I left her sitting in the rain. And now I search the truck stops off the beaten path. I watch the benches at the bus depots, the lunchroom counters and the on-ramps of freeways.

We live with the decisions we make.

Snap.

Threats and more

Ray Donner had been threatening to shank and stab Josh Cleveland for the past two weeks. It was getting on everybody's nerves. Other staff members had talked to him, asked him to stop the bullshit, to no avail. Whenever we attempted to redirect Ray, he would target another group home resident or staff member. He was a predator looking for another victim.

Ray Donner

Name: Ray Donner

Affect	Mood	Participation	Behavior
Worried	Labile	Cooperative	Compliant

Ray caught Josh Cleveland coming out of the diner, threw him against the hallway wall and leaned on him, pushing his own face to within inches of the kid's.

"You talking about me? I heard you was saying things. You got anything you want to say now, bitch?"

Josh stayed relaxed, watching Ray's eyes. It's all in the eyes. He said, "I been saying nothing about you. I don't even know you. I stay away from troublemakers, and that's what you are."

"You are a lying sack of shit," Ray spit, "And I am going to cut you a new one. Shank and bake, buddy. Grab and stab is what you are going to get."

I had just finished lunch and came out to find these two chest to chest in the hallway. And I don't give a damn, but somebody was going to get hurt. "To your rooms, both of you," I snapped. "I'll be along.

The foundation for improvement in Ray is questionable. His treatment program is faltering. He continues to have a hard heart and his treatment of others in the home has remained unchanged. He flips them off, cusses at them and threatens to kill them. He doesn't care about himself and has no interest in treatment.

He is supposed to be my one-on-one this holiday season. I am concerned about doing anything for fear of his behavior around family. I'm concerned about taking him out in public. His response is, "I don't care."

I think deep down he knows nobody really cares about him, so he "hardens his heart" and makes all the residents of the home pay for it. I've told him that if his attitude improved he might be able to move to another level of group home, less restrictive, but failure to work his program here means he might need a home with higher level security.

"What about the coping skills the therapists gave you," I asked. "How's that working out?"

He stated simply, "They're all gay. I'm not doing that crap."

This pattern of behavior is not good for this young adolescent. He knows nobody really backs him, so why try. He has no knowledge of or confidence in a good outcome. I told him he must make better choices but there is no one to support him.

Ray also struggles with stealing, believes stealing is essential for survival. He actually believes money allows a person freedom. He has no job skills, so steals instead. Anger is the elephant in the room.

Would you like to see my penis?

round 9 p.m. one December evening a few weeks before Christmas, Dez Morton asked another resident if he would like to see his penis. This resident then told me because I was standing in front of his doorway, though I wasn't able to hear the conversation. I discussed this with Mr. Craig, another staff member. Dez was asked to stop and he complied.

Dez Morton

Name: Dez Morton

Affect	Mood	Participation	Behavior
Intelligent	Stable	Cooperative	Compliant

he next day Mrs. Charlene asked me if I had noticed any changes happening with Dez. She said a resident had told her Dez was trying to show him his privates. The more we talked I realized Dez may have been acting out because of self-image problems. He might be going through hormonal changes and needed to talk to a therapist. I told him he might be victimizing himself by making poor choices about delicate issues.

Later, I visited with Dez about being careful not to become the abuser. I told him change is part of the process and talking with a therapist was a way of dealing with these changes.

This is a smart kid. At a group session he had more than enough examples and responses and was willing to share. Indeed, he was more than happy to talk the whole time if allowed. He told how he treated teachers at school during the week and what he valued. He looks up to Kobe Bryant, but in the next moment got sarcastic and said he also looked up to another resident because of his stealing prowess. I sat him down and told him I was disappointed.

That's the thing about Dez. He is smart and that leads to sarcasm and boredom in group at times. He has a big mouth and speaks out of turn. He thinks he knows it all.

When the group provides a challenge, he finds this enjoyable and shows great leadership abilities. There is something here that makes me worry. I think of the movie *The Lord of the Flies* and wonder if he may be the wrong leader for the pack.

Oklahoma Community Programs

The Halliday Group Home looked like a bureaucrat's cheap alternative, cinder block walls covered in green paint leftover from the Korean War. Originally it had been the Totter-Inn, an inexpensive alternative to the chain motels that sprang up around Tulsa, Oklahoma, in the late fifties, early sixties.

Now it was a cheap motel turned into a cheap group home for damaged kids. It was a level four facility. One more bad incident and the kid was thrown into level five, a dungeon with leg irons, sleeping on straw. Good enough for them, some would say. People, residents, don't want a group home in their neighborhood, so Halliday's was in what amounted to a mall. Women who went in to get their nails done down the block were always curious, watching the main door in hopes of catching a glimpse of a resident. Morbid curiosity kept their gaze on the door.

There were sixteen boys and sixteen girls at any given time. There were thirty-two staff members hired to cover all the shifts. Mrs. Santos was the boss, had her own office. Mr. Danner was the administration man, sometimes even wore a suit. He had his own office as well, though smaller than that of Mrs. Santos. I was a member of the supervisory staff, combination cop, therapist, parent, teacher, and janitor. Just don't get involved.

The building itself was U-shaped. There were two hall-ways, one for the boys and one for the girls. Each group had its own living room, separated by the administration offices. Each hallway was about fifty yards long, front to back of the building. The laundry room was located at the end of the hallway on the boy's side.

Therapy rooms were located at the far end of the girl's hallway. Everyone, girls and boys alike, walked past all of the girl's rooms to reach therapy. All the kids in the home knew who was getting what. Information at the home was power. And if you were the only one who knew something about another kid, if it was a real secret, you were master, he or she a slave. A predator feeds well on secrets, marrow.

Each hallway had to be cleaned and inspected daily in case of a possible government inspection by the Department of Human Services (DHS). The kids were responsible for clean-ing their own rooms. Each kid had their own way of cleaning. Some took pride in their work and the cleanliness of the room and others couldn't have cared less, if it were not for the urging of the staff members.

Some of the kids had issues, bad issues, complicated issues that wound around their brainstems and made them crazy. The rooms of those kids smelled of urine and steps would have to be taken daily to address the health concerns that came with the issues. Some of the rooms smelled like old food. The kids would hide food and forget about it. Some hoarded food.

All the rooms had posters with a positive quote for the kid to read and look at. The living room and the hallway had quotes painted on the walls.

It didn't miss being a prison by much. There was another cinder block building ten yards from the main compound. We called it the diner. Because it wasn't attached, the kids had to walk across the open space, pick up their plates and utensils, choose their meal (it was cafeteria style), and sit, all according to age groups and gender.

The food was definitely good enough to eat. On Saturday and Sunday mornings we often had pancakes or French toast, my favorites. The kids were the serving staff, and the diner was cleaned after each meal and nightly by the older kids.

Snap.

The International House of Pancakes

L ife should be fair. Life should be noble. Life is what you make of it. Life happens when you're planning for the future. Collateral damage. Unintended consequences. Shit happens. Some days he didn't seem to be able to think in complete sentences.

He had slept in the truck in the Wal-Mart parking lot in Cairo, Illinois. He could only stretch out diagonally, but the sleeper was comfortable. He kept the engine running, the air-conditioning on and the doors locked. The vibration of the truck joined the white noise of the engine and he slept.

The I-Hop parking lot was often filled with young travelers early in the morning. They kept to the edge of the lot and waved at cars leaving. Sometimes they stuck out their thumbs. Drivers with a full belly were more likely to stop for hitchhikers. David looked over the young people, watched from the truck for fifteen minutes, sighed and put the truck in gear.

Snap.

From the progress report of Tommy Jacobs

I t began with Tommy acting out in group. He was not participating. When I addressed this in front of the group he began to get angry. I attempted to let this go, but one of the kids said he started flipping me off and was being "inappropriate." When I tried to address this he said, "Fuck you." He stood up and walked toward Pupa Kelly.

Kelly confronted him as I quickly approached. Tommy yelled, "Fuck all the staff. I'll fucking kill you." With that he started punching and kicking at us. We, the staff, placed him in a CPI hold and put him on the floor. He kept kicking and we had to get his legs under control. After holding him down for about twenty minutes he began to calm down and process certain things. We sent him to his room and he started to cry, begging someone to kill him.

I knew his story. I would say Tommy's guilt over things his father had him do is his motive. His is a war to reconcile the things his father made him do and staff expectations. He has to deal with the wrath of his father, the abuse this man laid on this boy. He knows his father raped his mother. And, to make matters worse, his father forced him to have sex with his mother. Tommy was made to believe his father was always right.

Tommy is violent, abusive, easily offended and destructive. He ended up with bruises on his face and a nosebleed after the staff restrained him. But it should be noted he flipped his wheelchair and busted his head on the concrete outside the diner. He then picked up the wheelchair, slammed it into the concrete and screamed at the top of his lungs. Sometimes lunch is wet sawdust.

Walking out to death in the sunshine

Brian Thomas had anger issues. Like so many others, his is a struggle for survival. With staff protection he was able to reacquire social skills but his anger got in the way. Brian had issues outside of the group home. Visits to his family were suspended because it would take him days to readjust to the home. It was two steps forward, three back when this happened.

Brian Thomas

Name: Brian Thomas

Affect	Mood	Participation	Behavior
Angry	Agitated	Avoidant	Compliant

When we talked about boundaries, Brian wrote in his notebook. We all knew, when we talked about independence versus isolation, that Brian had no support group and would have trouble living on his own. He pushed ahead, had his reasons for living though they were not based in reality. He had courage but no sense.

In a way, Brian died because I was disappointed. He didn't handle group well that day, had issues that weren't related to the home. By the end of the session he was angry. He wanted to be discharged, had had enough of the home and its rules and was tired of the smells and the turmoil.

He exploded and left the session, slammed his way through the doors and kept right on going. Two of Tulsa's finest were just pulling up to the home when he went screaming and yelling out the door. They asked him to stop.

He flipped them the finger, reached into his jacket and they shot him dead. He bled out in front of the group home, the sun shining and the birds chirping.

Brian Thomas got his discharge.

Children pay the price

Working with children at a group home is challenging. You never really know what's in store when showing up for work. It could be a calm and easy shift, or it could very quietly turn into chaos with the cops being called. The volatility of the environment keeps a person on their toes. Personality differences and conflicts abound.

When I first started working at the group home, I was under the impression most of the kids were bad and couldn't fit into family environments or adopted families. I came to the job with a "smack down the bad kids and get them under control" attitude. I should have realized they aren't bad kids per se, they have only been through bad situations and scenarios that caused an abnormal outcome. This was often due to a lack of processing and understanding skills, and undeveloped social skills that might have helped.

Much of my thinking was dictated by reading their histories. They were gang members, pulled from their families for molesting a brother or sister, out of control because of mental health issues and many other reasons. I thought that, as long as they were controlled, everything would go as well as it could. Control is essential to helping them make good choices.

We had a kid who, as he grew older, saw his real future better than the staff did. He watched situations and thought about what could have been done differently.

He continually ran away from the group home and would go into the community and steal from others. This was his idea of survival. When he came back everyone would ask him why he did what he did. His answer was, "Nobody was teaching me to live and succeed."

Teaching him to succeed could lead to who knows what, but as I listened I thought I knew what he was saying, he knew it would take money to survive. No one was teaching him a way of making money. Nobody was teaching him a trade. Even when taught a way of making money he would steal. It was a psychological and physiological issue, habit forming, even though he had a choice. His brain was wired to steal. It was part of his upbringing and, therefore, fitting into society would have been tough at any time because of his emotional constructs from years of abuse.

He had been raised in a closet. It was the least of many horrible experiences that made up this boy's childhood. Nothing seemed to make any difference. He was released from the group home, eventually found guilty of rape and sent to jail. Short term success at the group home didn't mean long term success on the outside. Listening led me to start thinking in new ways. I began asking the question, "What can be done to set them up for victories once they move into society?"

I thought of the parallels between hunting and the dynamics of the group home. The eyes have it in both hunting and the home. Body language is a book to be read at the home. Body language is a dance between hunter and prey, with emotions the music. Physical changes mark the rut of the buck. Physical changes in young adults are the signposts of maturity. Group dynamics mark both the wolf pack and the pack in the home. There is hunting in the hallways of the group home and in the deep woods. It is the way of nature.

As I was working with abused and neglected children in the group home I realized a few things about them. They do not have a father or mother that is able to take care of their needs, hence the need for placement in the home. They all have some form of emotional or behavioral disorder that prevents them from succeeding in either family or foster family environments. They are all victims of some form of abuse or neglect. They all have improper or inappropriate boundaries. Developed over time, these are often the result of abuse or neglect.

I believe the program I worked for was able to implement a few things very well. These strategies enabled the children to build proper boundaries. They learned to protect their own boundaries and respect the boundaries of others. This prevented the transference of abuse. Instead of using defensive mechanisms for survival, they were instructed to use offensive mechanisms for success based on the teachings of Jesus Christ.

Operating in a Christ-like manner means being aware of the agreements each of us must make with our environment and others in order to be successful. The children who have gone through the program successfully were able to function at a higher level in foster care. The child's ability to respond properly to direction and take the proper course of action was the key to the program. The counselors were able to take the kids and produce a proper outcome in about eighty percent of the time.

Don't many of us have the same issues as these children? Everyone needs someone to truly care for us. We need someone who is genuinely interested in our advancement, someone who will share what they have learned in life, mentoring and trying to find and correct wrongs done to us so that abuse isn't passed down.

Once the seed of abuse has been planted it looks to grow in that person. The cycle has been started. The target of the abuse doesn't understand what has happened. Once abused, they tend to abuse others, not necessarily conscious that what they are doing is wrong. They are part of the cycle.

How many of us see this cycle and don't even think about it? Self-abuse. Isolation is a form of abuse. A person who is connected with others but has no boundaries is abusing themselves. What is the correct, proper way to live life free of abuse? The word of God and the teaching of Jesus Christ can lead us away from abuse and neglect and towards the path of love and life.

Working at a group home affected me, and you would hear this from others, by giving me a sense of purpose. I learned to focus on the future for the sake of others and then to speak to others about their development. I learned to consider how I am speaking and treating others. And I know now what these kids, these unfortunate kids, have gone through. I know and have had to look at my own abuse. On my journeys, I speak to others about my experiences, and when I do, I learn again. Still thinking about the home.

To be a successful hunter, you must possess . . .

My head was in the clouds. A deer was approaching and I had no clue. The deer had not broken one branch to alert me. I was facing the wrong direction, but fortunately I was on the other side of the tree and the deer couldn't see me. Also fortunately for me, I turned my head to look over my shoulder and "poof," he was there.

I couldn't believe this eleven-point, double-brow-time buck had gotten within twenty yards of me. No time for asking how he did that. I just went into, "How do I get my bow in hand without alerting the deer?" mode. How do I draw for the kill?

He was a slow browser. He'd take a few bites, then look up, take a few more bites, then move forward a couple more steps. As he kept moving forward and browsing, I was able to get my bow in hand. He slowly moved his head behind a tree and I drew my string back.

It all happened so quickly. Just as I came to a full draw, it was like his senses came into full alert. He came out from behind the tree that way, his ears twitching and his eyes searching for movement. Looking through the peep sight, I found the target and let the arrow fly. "Thwack!" My arrow hit his lungs. He ran fifteen yards and dropped.

Use all your senses in the hunt. Hearing the deer approaching is as important as seeing the deer. Hearing the deer approaching is a "get ready and get set up before he gets here" signal. In brush or thick cover know that the deer can't see you and will continue to walk. Get ready. Is it coming your way?

To be a successful hunter, you must possess:

- **Patience.** The ability to sit in a tree stand. Or on the ground. To stalk and move quietly, more slowly than the prey's eyes.

- **Control of your presence**. To move without noise. To stay in the game regardless of weather conditions or topography. To exhibit strength and endurance.

- **Mental agility**. When things go down, they go down quickly and you must be opportunistic to take the shot. The hunter and prey have connected. Go for a humane shot.

- **Perseverance.** The playwright Samuel Beckett said, "Fail, fail, fail again, better."

The sounds of silence

I t was never completely quiet in the group home at night. The building ticked as it cooled and the furnace or air conditioning system would cycle on and off, depending on the season. If you cocked your head and listened, you could hear the traffic on the street outside.

As staff, we were attuned to the smaller sounds of the darkness, whimpering and crying, furtive sounds of predators, squeals, giggles and sobs. There were things that go bump in the night. Sometimes whispers turned to screams.

But, for the most part, kids slept well, it was peace and quiet. I did a lot of walking on the night shift, much like the military. It was my job to keep the kids safe, to keep the predators at bay, to watch over the flock. In the ongoing battle between predator and prey, I was often the sheepdog.

I walked the dark hallways, watched for movement where there shouldn't be, smelled the urine of the carpet, and listened for sounds with my ear to the door of likely prey. Guarding the sleep of the innocent was my highest duty.

Night is when the kids are most vulnerable. They are afraid of the dark. Many of them ask for a staff member to sit by the door. Why? For safety. What does it develop? Trust. If everything goes well during the night and they wake up and see you guarding the door, they might trust you with other things of importance like emotions, nightmares and hopes. The door is a powerful barrier to the outside world. The outside world is a scary place when you don't know how to survive.

The stories of the night are different and dark. Kids try to harm other kids at night. Some try and repeat behaviors that are unacceptable, night or day. That is why they are at a group home in the first place. At night kids act out sexually with other kids. They throw temper tantrums regardless of the hour. The small wee hours of the night bring predators, sex, violence and escape.

Last night, a boy tried to take a toy from a smaller boy, stealing, and this needed to be stopped. A bigger boy was yelling and picking on a smaller boy, and this needed to be stopped. Then a staff member went too far and needed to be stopped.

Who is the predator and who the prey?

The Law of the jungle, continued...

Lair-right is the right of the mother.
From all of her year
She may claim
One haunch of each kill for her litter,
and none may deny her the same.

The girls are different ...

Rose Hanson came to her first group meeting with a poor attitude. She was initially unwilling to share ideas, but showed great insight once she was comfortable. She gets agitated at other's behavior. She is goal-oriented.

Rose Hanson

Name: Rose Hanson

Affect	Mood	Participation	Behavior
apathetic	Agitated	Passive	Oppositional

As is often the case with first-timers, Rose had an attitude, was unwilling to share ideas or participate. I'm not too concerned. I'll look for better participation in a few weeks. Rose is preparing for transitional living and to that end we were discussing ethical decision making, scenarios that might happen to us in the work environment. She responded well and her insight allowed for a great discussion.

Rose handled sessions on money management and financial terms and concepts. She became agitated at other's behavior in the beginning of the group discussion. Her attitude and perspective got better as time went on. She has set up good goals and is working to reach them. You know you are reaching someone when they actually begin to enjoy group dynamics.

But it's not all good

C hange is hard for some kids. When Ashley Warren's caseworker left for greener pastures, she left Ashley "mentally gone." Having a new caseworker has helped, but she has poor boundaries and needs to be redirected.

Ashley Warren

Name: Ashley Warren

Affect	Mood	Participation	Behavior
Hyper	Silly	Cooperative	Poor boundaries

I n executing a portion of Ashley's treatment plan, we discussed identifying permanent relationships as part of our lives and as part of the seven elements of independent living. We defined permanent relationships as those involving individuals who are able to stay in place and are healthy and stable while trying to pursue our life goals and dreams. She handled the discussion well even though she has poor boundaries.

At another session, we discussed using moderation in our choices and the ripple effect from this moderation. We also went over extreme addictive behaviors that are unhealthy.

Ashley becomes agitated and angry when she doesn't understand the problems being discussed. We tried setting goals. The idea was to identify one area of life where goals seemed appropriate and to find ways to achieve those goals. It is much like mile markers on a highway. She understands the concept but gets agitated about life's circumstances. Simply put, she has to learn to make better decisions.

Barbara Delaney and the beauty that was gone

This morning, I was asked to help with Barb Delaney. She had trashed her room and peed on herself. She has consistently acted out in the morning and before going to bed while on my shift. Here are some of my thoughts for therapeutic restoration while she is a resident here.

Staci Eldridge wrote that woman was made "in the beauty of God." John Eldridge wrote that man was created "in the image of God."

Here's my word formula: Human − God = Animals. Animals defecate as part of a daily routine, when they are scared (as in scared shitless) and when they die.

Barbara trashed her room and peed on herself for protective reasons. She is scared and unsure of how to reconcile herself to the environment of the group home. And she is unsure how to reconcile herself to the expectations of staff.

When I stepped into her doorway, I asked, "Barb, do you know what you are doing?"

She replied, "No."

I said, "Barbara, if I told you, would you believe me?"

She replied, "No."

She has no self-esteem and trusts no one. When I asked another staff member, Ms. Tiffany, what actually happens in the morning, she said, "Barb has nightmares, often screaming 'No, no, no." in her sleep."

Barb's rape by her father has affected her subconscious. The rape by the father has caused the wrath of the child. Without the relationship of a good God, she has reverted to being an animal.

To improve her habits and condition her to normality, someone must coach her towards the second quadrant—humanity held back by fear. The ultimate goal is the first quadrant—humanity's best. There she can live a better life in spite of her father's abuse, rape and wrath.

Now she goes to sleep scared and wakes up scared. She will continue to use defense mechanisms until she feels safe.

When she is given something to do and does that job well, she gets a little carried away. She is not sure how to handle being good. This goodness must be allowed to shine through to help her heal. She has been treated badly most of her life. Barbara knows bad; being good is a new experience for her.

She asks herself, "Do I need to protect myself from being good?"

Her inner beauty has been stolen. Her animal spirit will try to steal it back. She believes stealing her beauty back is the best way. A different reason may have a better outcome.

Further thoughts and writings about Barbara Delaney

A strand of three cords can work for someone, as well as against them. Let's consider these three strands a beginning: the wrath of the father, the abuse by the father, and the rape by the father. Three cords tightening on Barbara Delaney, causing harm and preventing restoration of herself.

Father was a predator, motivated by his sexual relations with his wife, Barb's mother. He was frustrated by the lack of intimacy with his wife. This led to his abusing his wife and turning his attention to Barb. Her mother either gave in or didn't. Despite the mother, or as payback, the father looked for another victim.

First, Barbara had to watch and listen to the wrath of her father. Then she had to watch and listen to the abuse of her mother. Finally, she had to endure the punishment her father meted out.

She has learned to deal with others as her father dealt with her. She hears what is happening, prepares for the abuse to come and does something abnormal to prevent the abuse she knows is about to happen.

Barb's mother accepted the rape of her daughter; at least it wasn't her. If Mother wasn't in the know, or didn't do anything about the abuse, then there are three more strands (cords) working against Barbara: jealousy of the mother, wrath of the mother, and being blamed for the wrongs of the mother.

The staff is attempting to help her. Father isn't here anymore. Can she realize this? Could someone guarding her door at night form a trust? I write this because the predator always enters through an opening, the door or the window.

It's no wonder she has been driven crazy. Let us drive her back to sanity. With some understanding of concepts and agreeable solutions, she could be shown a way back to health. Straighten out her mind and we subdue the animal.

Musings on caring, competence, and CPI

C aring too much can produce anger. Competency in overcoming anger is needed, as is forgiving, to produce a good outcome. We build our lives around words. The words we choose for our vocabulary can be used to build our life around. The right words, the right outcome.

CPI is a process that prevents injury to either client or staff member, and can escalate or de-escalate a situation. A breakdown in communication can lead to a need for CPI. If both parties, staff and child, can come to an agreeable solution before the escalation starts, an enjoyable outcome can happen. If there is not an agreeable solution, then there will eventually be an environment escalating towards hostility, and restraint will probably take place for reconciliation to occur.

The group home program is meant to help clients develop a sense of self, a sense of self-worth, a sense of self-esteem, and a sense of ownership. Like the stomach, kidneys and liver, the brain has a filtering process and when the brain has been abused, the filtering process doesn't work like it should.

It is up to the staff to figure out a way to reinstitute this filtering mechanism. The filter is a boundary. We should not allow thoughts to determine the outcome; we should let the words we write guide us. A pattern of words should dictate our choices. Good choices lead to good decisions; bad choices lead to bad decisions.

Talking 'bout your predator, talking 'bout your prey

When I was working at the group home, I used to draw these diagrams, maps of relationships, expectations, motivations and outcomes. The diagrams had stick figures, circles with quadrants, steps and arrows. At the bottom or top would be directions, circle A or B. Syllables danced like the Rockettes: realization, attributes, emotions, disciplinary, identifying, individual, motivating, victimization, psychology kicked up their heels.

Diagrams A and B represent the carnal nature of man. It's predator versus prey, the motives of the predator versus the

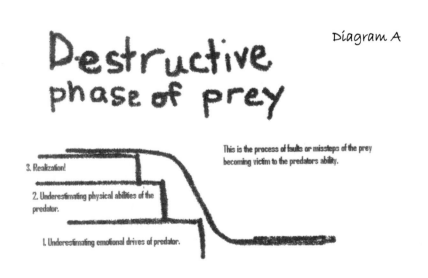

Destructive phase of prey

Diagram A

This is the process of faults or missteps of the prey becoming victim to the predators ability.

3. Realization!

2. Underestimating physical abilities of the predator.

1. Underestimating emotional drives of predator.

lack of knowledge of the prey. We're talking humans here. The goal of the predator is the victimization of its prey. To get there, the predator must go through a process of identifying the strengths and weaknesses of the prey. Think group home at night.

"What can I do to play off my prey's emotions?" asks the predator, "How can I overcome its physical attributes?"

The prey, not understanding, falls victim to the predator because, by the time he or she realizes what's been done, it's too late. The prey has not properly understood the motives of the predator, and has underestimated the emotional and physical attributes. The prey, the intended target, has been victimized. The sobbing is muffled.

Constructive phase of predator

Diagram B

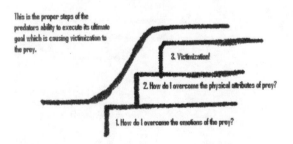

This is the proper steps of the predators ability to execute its ultimate goal which is causing victimization to the prey.

3. Victimization!

2. How do I overcome the physical attributes of prey?

1. How do I overcome the emotions of the prey?

Diagram C represents the ability of two individuals to build mutual respect for one another while understanding each other's motives. They teach each other, telling each other how they have been successful because of certain principles. Executing these principles has led them to become disciples, acknowledging different views.

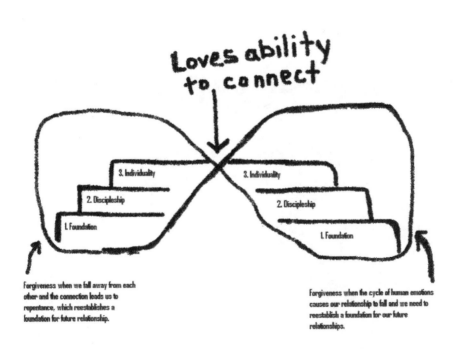

Constructive Connection in Christian Psychology

Diagram C

Loves ability to connect

3. Individuality

2. Discipleship

1. Foundation

3. Individuality

2. Discipleship

1. Foundation

Forgiveness when we fall away from each other and the connection leads us to repentance, which reestablishes a foundation for future relationship.

Forgiveness when the cycle of human emotions causes our relationship to fall and we need to reestablish a foundation for our future relationships.

I'm a predator, but it's just part of my job

I t all reads well on the page, looks good in a diagram. But Anthony Hagen is a welterweight spitting cobra. A predator in Keds. He has an ability to size anyone up, kids and adults alike. He marks and remembers victims like a squirrel buries nuts. I'm next on his list, I can tell.

He made progress for a little while, but I think he was testing the choices at a fork in the road. His is a cyclical violence. We were at the beginning of a cycle.

I remember the morning he asked to see me. He stood in the doorway for a moment, then decided slouching would be better and proceeded to take a pose against the doorframe.

I watched for a few minutes, then asked, "What would you like, Tony?"

He answered, "You failed."

I asked, "Failed what?"

He sneered, really, "My tests."

I replied, "Tony, you are a child and I am staff. I am in a position to recommend to Mrs. Santos whether you should stay here, go back to your mother's house, or be moved to a higher level security facility."

He thought for a moment and said, "I'm sorry."

Why was Tony testing me? Okay, so there might have been a reason, one of those unintended consequences. A couple of weeks prior to the "testing" questions, I had a thought about his problems and came up with a way to test how he handled disappointment.

What if he were adopted or put into a foster family and his family disappointed him, how would he react?

He had been asking me to take him to church for weeks. So I told him I would be happy to take him. We made plans, I encouraged him. That Sunday morning, I woke him up and told him we weren't going and that was that. It was a test, but he didn't know it.

He tried to rip me a new one, "You jerk. You son of a bitch. I hate you."

My point in sharing all this was to show that when young Hagen tested me, he showed an incredible understanding of human dynamics. He attempted, through self-promotion, to elevate himself to the same level as staff.

Showing his own understanding and applying his ability to empathize with others, he put himself in my shoes, caused a ruckus and, when I didn't react according to his predetermined outcome, informed me I had failed his test. What an ability for a fourteen-year-old. He has an instinctive gift, but uses it in a manipulative and destructive way.

If I had passed his test, it would have allowed him to perpetuate self-destructive behavior and put others at risk. Intelligence and a certain carnal ability make him a predator of the first rank. Is this kid playing us? Am I being too hard on him? How do we empower this kid to use his gift for a better outcome?

He is in a cycle of self-abuse, but is striking out and will hurt someone in the future. He capitalizes on other's weaknesses. He works with the program as an end to a means. His goal is to get back to Mom. He plays the game.

Bullshit is always part of the story

Joshua Cannady struggles with survival skills. On the other hand, he is upbeat and has a positive effect on his peers. Joshua handles anger well, unlike many in the home. He just doesn't handle reality.

Joshua Cannady

Name: Joshua Cannady

Affect	Mood	Participation	Behavior
POSITIVE	STABLE	COOPERATIVE	COMPLIANT

Mr. Terrell, an African-American staff member, and I were sitting in the hallway listening in on a conversation between Joshua and another resident of the group home. As they were talking, Joshua looked straight at me and said, "Mr. Dave, do you remember the time you took me hunting on the Arkansas River?"

He was trying to convince the other resident that I had taken boys from the home hunting. Everyone here knows I have not taken anyone hunting, nor do I have any plans to.

This was not the first time I had heard Joshua go off on a story he believes is true. I have overheard him do this a few other times, but when I corrected him and said I had never taken him hunting, he acted like he couldn't believe it. I asked Mr. Terrell if he had heard Joshua and he said he had.

My concern is that Joshua is going to tell more stories until he gets to the point where something needs to be addressed. He just does not handle reality well. He questions things he should realize naturally. He just doesn't "get" things he should at his age. I don't think he told that story to impress the other kid, but to convince others of a point he is trying to make.

Inside versus outside

Occasionally a kid would end up in the group home and we would have no idea why he was there. So it was with Robert Cohen. There was an adult somewhere in this kid, waiting to live his life. From his file, I learned he had been given up. His parents just called it quits, had better things to do.

Robert Cohen

Name: Robert Cohen

Affect	Mood	Participation	Behavior
POSITIVE	STABLE	COOPERATIVE	COMPLIANT

Often we would discuss the emotions many were having, the ones they were showing people versus the ones they kept on the inside. We talked about the conflict that happens when we do this, and the outcome that follows.

"Frightened" was the word Robert chose to describe the emotions he was feeling on the inside. He didn't appear frightened to the rest of us. For that, we used the word courage.

When we have courage, we do better in school, at the group home and in society in general. When I asked him why he felt no anger at being abandoned by his parents, he replied he knew they had problems of their own they couldn't seem to handle and he didn't blame them. That's maturity.

"Fuck this life" was carved into the boy's arm

I read the newspaper every day. When I'm home in Superior, I read the *Milwaukee Journal-Sentinel.* I should just stop. It doesn't do me any good and many times, it puts me in a black hole for the day. The group home story hit the papers about the middle of October 2015.

A former resident described the atmosphere in the home as chaotic. A transgender female was placed in a group home by the State of Wisconsin Department of Children and Families agent. She was a fifteen-year-old coming to terms with her sexuality.

"I walked through that door and it was crazy," said the young woman. She got into a fight within hours and fought every day after that. She reported sexual relations with an adult staff member and when workers outside the home found out, the police were called. She was kicked out the day after the police came to investigate.

The staff member's sexual activity included a fifteen-year-old boy who later hanged himself from a tree in the home's backyard. *Fuck this life* was carved into his arm.

There will be more charges brought against the ex-group home director. That'll help.

Predator, prey, and Jesus

'm a bow hunter. Hanging on the wall in my living room is one of my most treasured possessions. It is a stiff-necked trophy deer mount (shoulder mount) of a buck I call "Wis-key." I named him that because he is my "key" deer from "Wis"consin.

I was fortunate he walked in front of my stand on a beautiful October day. Before he showed up, I remember praying, "Lord, let me see a big buck before he sees me." The good Lord granted my prayer. Moments later, "Wis-Key" showed up.

His antlers were the first thing to catch my eye. He stood behind a jackpine about forty yards from my stand, moving his regal head from left to right. He began moving at a diagonal from north to south and crossed one of my shooting lanes. I used my thirty-yard pin and let loose the arrow. It was a double lung shot, fatal. He ran about ten yards and skidded to a halt. He never even knew I was there with him, didn't know what hit him. He had not a clue that I was there with him in the great Northwoods of Buffalo County, Wisconsin. I saw him go down and cried. As the saying goes, "Big buck down."

We are what we possess. Some possessions mean the world to us. We don't have to tell someone what these possessions are; they can see, hear, and read it in our life-styles. We choose what to do each day based on what we consider important. Come to my humble abode and you'll feel like you're in the woods, surrounded by ironwork trees, sun, moon, stars, birds and different animals. Eat at my table and you'll be served wild game on plates decorated with moose and hunting cabins. I live my heart's desire.

Jesus said we are to be the salt and light of the earth. That is our place in the world. When we share our knowledge and understanding with others, we give off light. By giving away, we assure our lives have meaning. We persevere through storms, wars, fights and conflicts. That's what the salt does. Are we taking our rightful place in the world? We must ask if what are we doing is right. What are we doing wrong? Why do we exist? Where are we going?

As Christians, what do we have to do to become America's treasure? Better yet, how do we become a world treasure? When we journey with Christ, others ask, "What do they have that I don't? How do I go about finding God?"

What are God's treasures? I would answer, "His Word, His Son, the Universe and man, both lost and found." He gave us His Word for direction. He sent His Son for us to know Him, and learn His ways. He gave us both authority and stewardship over the land and animals. He rejoices at those who are part of His kingdom, and celebrates when one who is lost finds his way.

Just as I have created an environment in my home for what I love, so God did the same. How much does He love us? He created us in His image so that we may pass His blessing from heaven to earth. First came the blessing. The blessing was passed down from Noah to his family, then from Abraham to Isaac, and from Isaac to Jacob. The blessing became the Ten Commandments. The need for another gift arose and God sent His only son, Jesus, to do what the commandments couldn't—show us what it means to be sinless.

What do we desire? Love, food, sex, shelter, and freedom would satisfy most of us—surface needs. If we're lucky, sex and love go together. Someone to be with, someone to be intimate with, something to eat when we're hungry, and the freedom to do what we want when we want to do it. That's the ticket to happiness.

Look around. Are we a happy bunch? I don't think so.

None of us are alike. We all have different desires. We have different political views, different experiences, different cares and desires. Good, bad, right or wrong, this is how it is in the kingdom of earth. Witness and testify to the chaos, drama, randomness and inequality. This is God's lesson after the fall.

Remember the fall? Remember Adam's first wife, Lilith? What would the world be like if Lilith had had her way? She wouldn't go along with God's plan to make her subservient, no stretching out under Adam. Lilith walked away from a bad deal and look what we ended up with. Adam and Eve. It could have been different from the start.

Come hither, young man

Predators sometimes wait in ambush. Other times, that same predator will just lift her skirt or unbutton an extra button on her blouse. Merrilee Williams was like that. She leaned over boundaries and waggled a finger or showed some cleavage. Plainly, she sought male resident's attention. It was tough to watch at fourteen.

Merrilee Williams

Name: Merrilee Williams

Affect	Mood	Participation	Behavior
Seductive	Anxious	Cooperative	Demanding

I know she was only a young woman, but Merrilee Williams flopped her can around with the best of them. She wrote notes to her boyfriend and when an old resident showed up for a visit, she displayed improper boundaries while grabbing the young man's ass.

On the other hand, she encouraged others, was socially responsible and exerted a positive influence on other members of the group.

Merrilee participates in group just fine. She is clear about qualities she would like to have and show to others. She chooses the heart as a metaphor for what she would like to be like. It keeps things flowing and is pivotal to life. The young woman is emotional at times.

She has trouble with boundaries. Merrilee is blatantly trying to seduce a male resident of the home and is caught up in seeking, demanding that male resident's attention.

Finally, she has seemed to come to grips with her sexuality, but in her case, that means comfortable. Other than that, she is setting better goals and thinking of college. Merrilee understands it is up to her.

Some people might as well wear a sign reading, "I am prey."

We have all seen it in our lives, a caring person is made the butt of jokes, embarrassed in public, made fun of at home. A caring person is often treated like crap.

Anita Donovan

Name: Anita Donovan

Affect	Mood	Participation	Behavior
Positive Bright	Stable Agitated	Cooperative Avoidant	Compliant

Might as well hang a sign on her. Anita Donovan is a very caring person, and gets treated like crap because of it. She needs more confidence and she needs to become aware of her environment. She just doesn't see the blow coming.

She's a participant, but is learning avoidance. Where she used to offer encouragement to others, she is now more hesitant. She gets frustrated at group dynamics, but still tries to lift up some of the other girls. She has great insight and is developing goals for herself.

In the words of Dr. Steven Covey, "Seek first to understand, then to be understood." If she can just make it out of the group home alive, she should do fine.

We live in a society where education is looked down on and caring is a fault.

Cowboy with a gun. That's our hero.

She wasn't the only one.

S ome fifteen-year-old girls look about ten. Others are mature beyond their years with the moves and looks of a vixen. Angie Bauer once confronted me in the hallway, put her hands on her hips, licked her lips, stared at my crotch and said, "You got a blue pill, old man? I got the time."

Angie Bauer

Name: Angie Bauer

Affect	Mood	Participation	Behavior
Worried Seductive	Stable	Cooperative	Compliant

A ngie's participation in group was good. She shared with the group that she would like to have the qualities of a wolf, be part of a pack. Little did she know. Angie was constantly on the prowl, protective and offensive at the same time. She said she was ready to get out there and begin living her life. She shrugged her shoulders provocatively and admitted she liked being up at night.

Baloney, she reveled in being up at night. She also kept trying to size me up. I was never sure whether she was being sarcastic.

Angie had anger issues as well. We discussed ways to reduce her anger.

The Law of the Jungle, continued...

The kill of the pack is the meat of the pack.
Ye must eat where it lies;
And no one may carry away
of that meat to its lair, or he dies.

Pushing buttons.
Life's choices can either lead to more life or get us killed. It's as simple as that. Sometimes the choices involve words, sometimes actions. Sharon Ripley's anger makes her impulsive. Sharon cooperates but, to be honest, her anger comes to the surface when she realizes she can't control the behavior of others. Good luck on that.

Sharon Ripley

Name: Shelly Rockley

Affect	Mood	Participation	Behavior
Apathetic	Silly Irritable	Passive	Manipulative Oppositional

The movie *Lord of the Flies* is a great teaching device. It's easy to identify the maturity level of the kids in the movie and link it to what happens to the kids in the home.

We talk about how we are to mature over time. Maturity means following a leader, but the wrong leader can mean death. Maturity means identifying abusive cycles or patterns. Sharon can identify abuse, she has seen it in the night at home, but cannot seem to walk away from abusers. It seems constructive relationships are harder to identify and sustain.

Anger often comes from sources that have affected our lives. We are often hurt by those we love. They push our buttons and we are unsure how to communicate our anger. Smart and angry make a potent cocktail.

Dictionary

I t was day 12 of two weeks on the road. I had settled in, the Peterbilt was home, refuge, and all I had was what I carried. I tried to be clean, but I was reminded of a hamper in the locker room.

I keep a small pocket-sized dictionary in the truck and try to work on my vocabulary regularly. I was trying to work *ennui* into everyday conversation. The waitress this morning looked at me like I had a speech defect.

So, twelve days means a certain weariness, *ennui*. At home, I sometimes haul out my two-volume, boxed set of the *Compact Edition of the Oxford English Dictionary*. The books are huge, the type so small a magnifying glass is included, tucked into its own drawer. When I'm home, I like to get comfortable in the kitchen with the big dictionary and my Bible.

I like to have a beer occasionally, but drink at home mostly. I'm not home enough to want to leave when I get there. So I open a bottle of beer. I like glass bottles. St. Pauli Girl is my favorite of late, but my backup is Miller High Life. Maybe it has to do with the girls on the labels. I'm going to have to look up *dirndl*.

"Hey, over here, I'm a drama queen..."

helley Rockley is her name. Shelley wasted her time in group doodling on a piece of paper. When Tremaine Washington made a comment she didn't know how to handle, Shelley went silly. She told me Tremaine passed notes when I wasn't looking. I believe this was in response to how Tremaine made her feel about one of her answers. She's a very bright young woman who allows another person to affect her.

Shelley Rockley

Name: Sharon Ripley

Affect	Mood	Participation	Behavior
Bright	Stable Angry	Cooperative	Compliant

roup went very well until the end of the session when Shelley started arguing with Angie Bauer. Creativity and enthusiasm are hallmarks of every drama queen. I have asked her to handle herself better so that she doesn't face consequences for acting out. The next session she did fine, almost starting something, but backing off in the end.

Shelley continues to push limits and test boundaries, acting out in a childish manner.

Sometimes in the hallway

Sometimes we journey back to what seems like a brighter yesterday so we don't have to think about our dark todays.

Sometimes the memories are so dark we are loath to enter those rooms of yesterday where old clocks tick.

Hallways bother me now. I have a house. All those closed doors on the hallways of apartment buildings. At night in the home, I would walk the threadbare carpets and listen at the doors, cheap wooden doors. The wood of the doors was always warm and steeped in the smells of the home, hormones and young sweat, testosterone, unwashed clothes and deeper, fear.

I would place my ear against the door and listen to the rhythms of masturbation and the mewling of babies in teenage bodies who were afraid of the new person moving in. Some wanted to stay children, though that had provided no shelter. Old pain, familiar pain was better, known, had been lived through.

Teen years brought longings and aches, growth spurts and voice changes, pimples and boils and flashes of anger that heated the body.

Sometimes the listening found whispers and soft singing. Lullabies, I thought, until the singing became chanting, "Penis, penis, you've got a little penis."

Then there were the muffled sobs. When I kicked through the door, the feral smiles on the faces of the boys turned to frowns. They broke for the corners of the room and I took the girl into my arms. I backed out the door with her and moved into the hallway. I locked the boys in the room and yelled for staff.

Mr. Devlin and I unlocked the door once Mrs. Santos had taken the girl to the office. We watched the boys. Two did as they were told and moved to the hallway. We had to take down the other two. Sometimes violence was a pleasure. These boys seem to think cage fighting is just another level of conversation.

Don't they just reflect the coarsening of our society? From politics to religion, it's kicks and bare knuckles. Other countries think of themselves as "we." America thinks only of "me."

More Law of the Jungle

When ye fight with a wolf of the pack,
ye must fight him alone and afar,
Lest others take part in the quarrel,
and the pack be diminished by war.

Predators arrive in white vans

A few new kids arrived with both poor boundaries and a history of gang-related abuses. One kid had been raped by gang members. Another had highly aggressive sexual issues. The other kids were low-IQ placements and African-Americans. It was like giving squeaky toys to the wolves.

It all started with a quick glance at breakfast. I looked at one of the new kids and we had a quick conversation. I sensed the new kid didn't like me but I didn't know his history. He sucker-punched me while I was trying to pick him up off the floor. That's another story. I figured the punch wasn't going to be the end of it. It wasn't.

The kid must have made friends because the following events took place not long after he arrived. When it was my turn to take over the hallway from another staff member, the kids watched to see when the first staff member left. One staff member always left 15 to 30 minutes early, which meant I was in the hallway by myself. I didn't have a problem with this; most of the kids were already asleep and in bed. Those awake and watching were the ones I worried about. They were the ones prone to plotting and attacking, looking for an opening. As time went on, they knew when I would be isolated, alone.

The first test came when I was redirecting a child. The child said loudly, "Come get Mr. Dave." I heard footsteps behind me. Prepared for the worst, I turned. But it was the new kid quickly shuffling his feet in place, making as if he were running. He wanted to see my reaction. He didn't actually want to attack me, not just then. I did what anybody would do who was concerned with the dynamics of the situation; I brought it to the attention of another staff member, one higher in authority. He handled it the best he could, but it wasn't going to be over soon.

As the week went by, I got a horrible feeling in my gut. Something was planned for the weekend when I would be isolated, and it would not have a good outcome. Something was not quite right, but I couldn't explain it. My supervisors thought I was crazy. I decided to take events in my own hands—I took a vacation, and had a blast.

When I came back the following week, it was evident that four or five of the black kids had been planning on jumping me in the hallway when I was alone. The leader of the group home said they had "racist" issues and that there were other things that needed to be addressed. We were put on high alert. Some good conversations came out of this situation and the staff gained some respect for each other. We began looking out for each other in earnest.

One morning, I was watching the younger boys in the living room. Something didn't seem right. We had a new employee and things didn't seem to be flowing like normal. I didn't hear anything, but went back to make sure everyone in the hall was doing what they needed to be doing to get all the kids into the living room.

When I came into the hall, I found a staff member up against the wall with a kid wildly throwing blows to his face and body. The staff member had his hands up to protect himself from the blows, the flying fists of fury.

The staff member was in shock and unable to move. I quickly threw off my glasses, knowing I might have to take a hit to get the kid off the staff member, then leaped into action. I came from the kid's side and threw my arms around him, then put him in a bear hug. The other staff member and I put him into a restraint hold until the kid came to his senses. I had gone a little far to fix the situation.

Snap.

Bobby Martin talks

obby Martin lay curled on his bed. He talked into his pillow, "I can't talk out loud. I whisper. Even then they hear me.

"I look when I can. They mustn't see me looking.

"I don't have to raise my head to smell. I've learned a lot from smelling. Fear smells like urine.

"I keep my hands in my pockets. I know I mustn't touch. I know the word *mustn't*.

"Taste. I've been told I wolf my food. Taste is secondary."

A leader for good

Tremaine Washington identified qualities he would like to be: brave, courageous and bold. Here's a kid who identifies with the group.

Tremaine Washington

Name: Tremaine Washington

Affect	Mood	Participation	Behavior
Positive	Stable	Cooperative	Compliant

Tremaine is attentive, forgiving and patient. He would make a good counselor if he could stop his lying habits. He shows leadership by giving advice to others about boundaries and things not to do. Good advice about not getting a girl pregnant before being able to handle it. Tremaine is still aggressive towards female residents.

There's a lack of ambition here

Moderation in all choices, that's my motto. There are ripple effects from moderating our choices. Chuck Stratton. There's a point where you know he hears all the right words, but will he apply them? That's where this kid is at. He responds.

Chuck does not understand what maturity is. After watching *Lord of the Flies* in class, the group was asked to provide a list of morals they would like to live their lives by.

Chuck got angry. When asked to talk about abusive relationships, Chuck shut down. But he became intrigued by the conversation the group had about anger. We talked about how anger can produce a hostile environment that is not safe for ourselves or those we love.

They hooked up

Our group sat at the table discussing independent life skills. The two kept looking at each other with big fawn eyes. It's in the eyes. I asked them to stay focused on the discussion, and they did. However, at a group home, anything can happen after a look like that. It is the look that passes between a teenage boy with raging hormones and a girl who wants to be loved.

At the time, I couldn't say what their plans and intentions were; I only knew I should inform other staff members they were looking at each other and something might go down.

Go down it did.

One thought it was love—the girl. And one did it for bragging rights—the boy. And boy, did he brag about it! The consequences included a diagnosis of a sexually transmitted disease, STD. One was a carrier and the other got taken.

It should be noted this incident did not happen on the property. Sex between residents was strictly forbidden.

One of the case histories

O f all the boys in the home, there was one man. Granted, the man lived in the body of a boy, seemed a boy, and looked like a kid who flew balsa-wood airplanes. The man who lived in the boy filed his teeth to points.

I thought long and hard about making work at a group home a career. But the lives of the kids, their histories and what I saw each day curled like feral dogs in my head. I tried not to wake them up.

One, two, three, four, five

H earing.

I heard things, listened to how the boys and girls pimped each other in the diner, dissed each other in the hallways, and threatened each other in the shadows. There were sounds, not even formed into words, designed to disrupt, scare, startle and intimidate. Barks and growls from the darkness worked on the smaller kids.

Catch someone's eye and you don't need to make a sound to threaten. Little gestures make a bully. Point a loaded finger and pull the trigger. Cut your throat from ear to ear with that same finger. Look daggers. Stare. Day or night, darkness or light, it was in the eyes. Goodness, cunning, fear and anger live in the eyes.

Smells. To this day, I smell urine where there is none. I don't like to see carpet in a dining room. The faintest whiff of pee and I am back at the group home, watching over my shoulder.

What other odors take me back? Shit, sweat, body odor in general, really cheap teeny-bopper perfume—all take me back. The smell of cooking gas in the diner. Old grease.

The sense of touch can take me back as well. Threadbare sheets and blankets. Chipped Formica tables. Pebbled plastic chairs. Plastic plates and silverware.

Taste. The copper taste of blood.

Another hunting story

The river bottom had a line of telephone poles running parallel to the river. There was a clearing for the poles and on either side, the forest was thick. I found a trail and set up my tree stand about fifteen feet up. Opening day, I climbed up into it. Late in the day, I started hearing noises from the tree line. I thought, "Oh boy, here we go." I picked up my bow and waited. A really good eight-pointer came sniffing my way.

I had already drawn my bow when I realized he was sniffing the air, looking for me. All of a sudden, our eyes met. He froze and I took aim at his vitals and released the arrow. I ended up hitting him in the spine because he tried ducking. He went down. I followed through with another arrow for a humane kill.

Can deer see what I see? No. Can they hear what I am hearing? Yes. Can they smell what I can? Yes. Am I seeing what they see? No. Can I hear what they are hearing? Yes. Can I smell what they can? No. Our sense of smell is not close to that of a deer. And deer are smarter than we give them credit for.

So are kids.

How I learned the meaning of fair chase

I once killed a doe in the wee small hours of the morning. That little deer actually knew I was in the tree stand.

I had been hunting over bait, a pile of corn set out to attract deer. The doe heard me come into the woods. She thought I had brought food. She approached and I shot her. But as I looked back on the situation, I realized I hadn't hunted the deer. That deer was hungry. I took advantage of her hunger and killed her.

In my ignorance of baiting, I actually thought the deer was just walking my way as part of her daily routine. But this was far from the truth. The doe had come in thinking I had put out bait; when the bait wasn't in its normal location, the deer looked up in the direction of the tree stand right before I killed her.

I told myself, after that day, I would never bait a deer and hunt like that. I can't say that about bear, but I'll never hunt deer over bait again.

I really felt bad. It had been a hard winter and this doe was looking for a handout from someone she thought was a friend. I was the friend; I had been feeding the deer and that's why she showed up. But I was there to put meat in my freezer; I was not a friend. It was a misunderstanding on the deer's part.

It is better to hunt with a fair chase in mind, where it takes skill to take the animal, than to kill it the way I did. It was an insult to the deer. It came in friendship, only to die.

It takes skill to hunt. It takes knowing the habits of the animal, what it eats, where it beds down for the night, the trails it moves on through the woods. Then you are a predator, a hunter at the top of the food chain. Shooting a bear over apples and donuts or a deer over corn only makes you a killer, a murderer. It's nothing to be proud of.

As long as I'm on a philosophy rant, let me speak to what I consider one of my cornerstones. I believe in working toward principled outcomes. Our beliefs must guide our actions. It's important to be centered, and to use this as a base for doing good works. That's simplistic. Let's say we must work to educate ourselves, then use this education to shape our beliefs, and then act.

It's one thing to theorize in the cab of a truck in the middle of the night, another to put theories into action when a woman takes the seat at the counter next to you. My first reaction was not to notice. Five years later, the young woman I had left in the rain, the young woman I had looked for at every truck stop and shelter, took the stool next to me and changed my life.

I like to think it was because of a life lived with principles. Snap.

Mr. Devlin, staff member and co-worker:

"What you got with Mr. Dave was a six-foot-two-inch naïve young man. This fellow did not have a clue, Army M.P. or not. He'd wade in with Jesus like some parrot on his shoulder. I swear somebody was whispering to Mr. Dave all of the time. And he was answering. I'm not saying it was bad; he did well with the kids.

"Like so many who work in group homes, he was damaged himself. But it made him better. He tried harder because of his past. He was a good guy to work with, had your back without a doubt.

"Mr. Dave was pretty much in control, directed toward a principled outcome. That was his phrase and by the time he left, we all knew what it meant.

"There was a deep sadness in the guy as well. He looked into my eyes, looked at my face to see if I was the one. I wasn't, but I'd like to think I was okay in his eyes."

It can't happen here

We watch the show where the predator waits in the kitchen. We aren't sure who are the good guys, who the bad. Who is the predator, who the prey? Isn't this exciting? What is the husband going to do to his wife? What did she say to antagonize him? Is there a gun in the house? This could be good.

Our well of love is not bottomless. When we are out of love, we are no longer in God's kingdom, the kingdom of the heart. What we have left is the carnal nature of man— sexuality, immorality, impurity, lust, evil and greed. It all sounds like fun, great and tempting, but leads to death. The effects are evident: anger, rage and hate.

Without love, couples in a relationship start taking advantage of each other, abusing each other. But a relationship does not need to be one of predator and prey. We can lead a life where the blessings of God are transferred to us, and our inheritance and promised lands are restored.

How many individuals who have suffered abuse or neglect really understand what it is to be blessed? It's obvious that being blessed is the opposite of being cursed. But what happens when we fall just short of the blessing, when our heart's desires are not being met? We often resort to a predator-prey relationship to get what we want.

Doesn't being blessed mean we are sharing in Christ's riches? Yet we feel we are missing out when we compare our possessions to those of someone else. Being blessed is a jagged little pill and hard to swallow. The Ten Commandments ensured God's blessing.

Love makes the world go 'round.

Love is what you need.

We love the Lord. We start to use His name to bless people. We start seeing how everything He created is holy, of a piece. We learn to love, honor and cherish our families. We stay committed in our relationships. We give away. We remain open and honest and learn to love others and protect what is theirs. What began in our spirit becomes part of our reality.

When we let God into our lives, we must consider motive in our day-to-day activities. Prioritizing is key, as is making preparations to take us to the final destination. Ask yourself, "Did I do something constructive at the end of the day? What did I accomplish?"

We inspect our work, our possessions and examine ourselves. We become "blessing" minded and realize spirituality is our true source of strength. Blessing is a commodity. The more we use it the bolder we grow, the more capable we become. We are able to pull off things once thought unattainable. By faith, we come to our completion.

Writing this book is the only thing in my life I can construct that nothing will be able to destroy. They say the pen is mightier than the sword. Also, Jesus said heaven and earth would pass away, but his words would not. Why not? Because John said, "In the beginning was the Word, and the Word was with God, because the Word was God." As long as my words reinforce God's word, they cannot be destroyed.

A Christian soldier

David is a man of his time. As he says, "First a Christian, then a soldier." He weighed in at over seventeen stone and stood six feet two inches tall in his wool socks. He had a heart of gold and the guilt of a good Catholic, but he was a Holy Roller through and through. At times, David wielded the outrage of the Old Testament without a governor, and that got him in trouble.

He might as well have been Muslim with the lashings he gave himself. Ask his therapist in Iron Mountain. She told him, "Amp up your curiosity, David. Sometimes you should be glimpsing hope. What are you curious about?"

Where does hope come from? To David, hope never seemed a religious term, exactly.

He was listening to Joe Ely when he downshifted coming into the Memphis city limits. He had made sure the Peterbilt could play old technology. The vinyl he collected he stored at home in old fruit boxes. He burned CDs from the old vinyl. Part of his trip-taking routine was going through tapes and CDs and packing tunes to match the trip.

Ely was a storyteller and, to David, his voice spoke the pain of relationships, old lovers and enemies. He often packed Mason Ruffner, Delbert McClinton, Robbie Robertson and liked the Almond Brothers. But it was Roy Buchanan who got him up. One of his favorites was *The Messiah Will Come Again*. It shows you can pray with a guitar.

Electricity

've learned I don't really like electricity, and it's not just because I stuck a key in the wall socket when I was three years old. I have it in my house; it came with the place. The house I bought near Superior came with an old Monarch wood stove as well. Its bulk fills the kitchen, and when stoked in the morning, it radiates heat. Flames glow in a red circle around the old enamel coffee pot. I keep the wood box filled with pine and oak I chop myself.

In the fall, when ducks and geese, mallards, black ducks and Canadians fill the skies with their calls, I go hunting. I kill only to eat and eat what I kill. I shot two mallards last Saturday morning and let me tell you, the Browning 12-gauge is a fine gun. I have a Belgium model from 1954. Two shots.

I sat at the kitchen table and spread newspaper. I plucked the feathers from the ducks and laid them side by side on the funny pages, which are not the same as when I was a kid. I read *Prince Valiant*.

When I got back from hunting, I built up the fire in the stove and set an old soup pot filled with paraffin wax from last season on to heat. I got it to just below boiling, then picked up each duck by the head and lowered it into the wax, coating the entire body. Sank one duck at a time. Then I laid them back on the paper and removed the pan of wax from the heat.

It didn't take long for the wax to harden. Then I peeled the wax off. The hardened wax took the pinfeathers with it, leaving a baby's butt of duck.

I got the oil lamp from the cupboard, lit it and put it in the center of the table. After cleaning the ducks, I put them in the old, blue, enamel baking pan, sliced both an apple and an onion and stuffed them into the ducks. I wrapped the birds in bacon and put them in the oven.

No electricity. I went to the mantle in the living room and lit another oil lamp. The evening closed in. I heard a jay in the birch tree next to the porch and the neighbor's dog howling down the road. I watched the yard turn blue in the dusk. I could smell the ducks from the porch.

Thoughts passing through Dubuque

Is cruelty a given? Daycare, preschool, kindergarten, grade school, junior high, high school, college. Come over to the frat house for a party?

Churches, retreats, pedophiles, preachers, priests, pastors, don't forget the nuns.

South America, Central America, North America, Africa. The Catholic church deemed all the inhabitants "sub-human."

Name an institution that is safe. Home?

People who have been mauled by a predator look at the world askance, listen with severity and never knew a promise that wasn't broken.

Temptation and the List

One night, long ago in Tulsa, I sat at my plywood and Formica kitchen table, notebook in hand and three number two pencils within reach.

The parking lot of my apartment building stretched into the near distance, filled with trucks and cars of the young; plastic Pontiacs no longer made, Jeeps of dubious reliability and pickup trucks. Ram, Ford and Chevy mostly. Mine was the oldest, a lime green 1977 Ford F-150.

Farther in the distance, I could see the Cimarron River, civilized by a small park on its bank. There was one gift that came with the apartment—a view of sunset in the west, sometimes a darkening in the clouds, sometimes a clear orb sinking. It was not enough.

I made a list. A life has to be lived correctly. There is a design. I made a list of those things I needed. I thought of it as a bucket list, but realized it was a list for living. I figured if I could list the things I considered important in life, maybe I could narrow down the places I wanted to consider moving to.

1. *Keep the truck.*

2. *Buy land.*

3. *Hunt for food: deer, grouse, ducks, geese, coyote, bear, cougar, moose, elk.*

4. *Fish for all species: musky, northern, small and large mouth bass, catfish.*

5. *Eat real food, grow food or join a CSA.*

6. *Heat with wood.*

7. *Use kerosene lamps.*

8. *Cook over a wood stove.*

9. *Should have four seasons.*

10. *There should be lakes, rivers and big water.*

11. *It should be easy to travel from—East, West, North and South.*

12. *There should be opportunities to work and grow.*

13. *I'm looking for good people.*

14. *There should be access to colleges and universities.*

15. *No one should know my name.*

16. *The politics of the area should reflect my own.*

17. *I'm looking for a complex ecosystem.*

18. *Access to music, good radio stations and live music venues.*

19. *It should be an interesting "place" to live. For instance, the Superior area of northwestern Wisconsin is close to the Arrowhead region of Minnesota. Lake Superior is big water and the Upper Peninsula of Michigan has the Porcupine Mountains and the Keweenaw.*

20. *There must be quiet.*

21. *I am looking for a woman.*

22. *I need access to history and other cultures.*

23. *I will need a church to attend.*

24. *The cost of living, rent, food, health care must be affordable.*

25. *Access to public lands is important.*

26. *Restaurants*

27. *The young woman, Reb.*

There was that temptation, number 27. I wanted to know you, who you would become. But you had to get there yourself. That's what I thought.

I am walking away from a steady job, an apartment and the place of my growing up, the streets I've known, the nods and glances, groves of trees and front porches, backyards and apples, fishing and bare feet, crushes and touches, riding cardboard and berry picking, movies and storefront dreams.

Everything I had is gone. Now I guess I don't mind that a bit. I drove my pickup to the river and wept, adding my tears to the flowing water. My broken furniture is yesterday, that plasterboard apartment with its Formica table and Naugahyde couch.

I fit everything I am into the bed of my pickup truck, covered it all with a tarp. Everything I am is in cardboard boxes, duffle bags and gun cases.

Goodbye to my young woman in the rain. I am leaving it all behind. All signs point toward Superior, Wisconsin.

Home...

I have a house now and Wis-key is on the wall. I drink my coffee from an oversized mug with two pacing black bears painted under the glaze. My steak knives have bone handles and my dining room table is made from old barn planking. It wasn't always that way.

My apartment in Tulsa was two miles from the group home. I swear the carpeting in the hallway came from the same roll as the group home. Coming home smelled the same as going to work.

I've got a queen-sized mattress. A guy can hope. There's that word again—hope.

I never prayed I'd find her. I hoped. I never pictured anything afterward. I looked for her those years because I wanted to find her, to save her maybe, to protect her. That's what I figured a relationship was. I protect her and make decisions for her, show her what a Christian man can offer.

Who knew I was so far off base. Who I finally found was not the person I was looking for. I thought I was searching for a damaged young woman who needed help, who didn't have the skills to survive, who would welcome a mentor.

She as predator

Rebecca knew the moment she saw him. She just flat out, God-damn knew. From that moment on, he was a jackrabbit, making flying right angles in the snow, dodging claws. She was coming to save them both. Who knew it would take years.

She tracked him without fanfare. Once she found out David had moved out of state, the search became harder. Rebecca slipped away from the group home in the morning rain, found her friend Mina and took the spare bed in her room. Mina's Mom gave the okay.

Rebecca mopped floors, washed bathrooms, cleaned windows and dusted, but hard looks and scowls accumulated on Mina's mother's face. Reb was asked to leave. She was leading Mina astray. Reb made it last until two months after her eighteenth birthday.

The time had been well spent. With the money she had saved from waitressing a few hours a week, she took a bus to the twin cities of Minneapolis-St. Paul. A friend in the group home had done a little digging for fifty bucks.

Mrs. Santos had let drop that Mr. David had gotten out of the group home business and was driving truck long-haul and was maybe working in St. Paul.

St. Paul is a college town. Reb found work at a T-shirt shop near Macalester College and paid for a small bedroom in a student three-story Victorian.

She had stopped for breakfast at Mickey's Diner before catching the bus to the Como Park Zoo when Dolly Johnson sat down next to her.

Now she rode shotgun for Three Roses Trucking. She wore a pair of black Harley-Davidson boots, black jeans and a blue Snakestretchers T-shirt. There were two rings on the middle fingers of each hand and two studs in the lobes of both ears. No other jewelry was attached to her body.

She wore bangs, as she had at the home. She wasn't tough, but gave the impression of maturity.

Iceland

watched one of the news channels last night. There was a short piece about Iceland—no army, no guns, very little violence, not much crime, and great productivity. It turns out the whole country is atheist. Without religion, would it be a peaceful world? So asks the truck driver crossing the plains of Canada in the middle of the night.

The Other

I f you are "the other," you are prey.

For the Israelis, this means the Palestinians.

For Europeans, it is now the Africans.

For the Americans, it is the Mexicans, the Hondurans, the Guatemalans, the Salvadorians, the Panamanians and all the other wetbacks. It used to be the Spics, Bohunks, Polacks, and Niggers of all shades.

Cast them as stupid, smelly, mongrels and it's a lot easier to make them slaves, have them work for pennies, deny them rights and schooling, restrict them from voting.

And build a wall to keep them out.

Talking 'bout the Book and the Word

I spend much of my time alone. Driving long-haul is a singular business and I live alone. I don't have a dog and cats are just yucky. It's said talking to yourself is okay as long as you don't answer.

I carry both ends of a conversation with aplomb. I have my own take on many subjects, including religion, but I'm open to a good argument. Sometimes I provide a good argument myself.

On a rainy night in May, I was parked in a rest stop outside Lexington, Kentucky. Our country is going to hell in a hand-basket. Some think the basket is full of dead babies. Wicked men sit with folded hands and wait.

Isaiah 32:7: The scoundrel's methods are wicked,
and he makes up evil schemes to destroy
the poor with lies, even when the plea of
the needy is just.

Look around you in this year of our lord 2016. Scoundrels are everywhere and the pleas of the needy have turned to sobbing. The poor are to use their bootstraps to pull themselves up, yet they have no boots. Those who have say with straight faces, "I started from nothing and you see what I have." They won't admit to their bashing and bullying, can't see a difference in abilities or why that would make any difference.

Jeremiah 5:26-28: Among my people are wicked men who lie in wait like men who snare birds and are like those who set traps to catch men.

Like capes full of birds, their houses are full of deceit; they have become rich and powerful and have grown fat and sleek. Their evil deeds have no limit; they do not plead the case of the fatherless to win it, and they do not defend the rights of the poor.

Politicians from mayors to presidential candidates, CEOs, judges, generals, cardinals, bishops and everyday priests are evil. Don't forget pastors, fathers and mothers, neighbors, teachers; they have forgotten the way.

Dn 12:10: Many will be purified, made spotless and refined, but the wicked will continue to be wicked. None of the wicked will understand, but those who are wise will understand.

And will those who are wise rise up? Many of those who are wicked have chosen that path. Many have been urged to that path by others, damaged and bent on passing the damage along.

Isaiah 29:20: Although the Lord gives the bread of adversity and the water of affliction, your teachers will be hidden no more, with your own eyes you will see them.

So who's the predator here? With all the adversity and affliction in the world, how can we be sure the Lord doesn't get a kick out of pain and suffering? The Catholic church, the church of Christ, Peter and Paul, the only true church, decreed the inhabitants of the new world sub-human, no better than animals. The better to take advantage. See if you can spot the real teacher.

> *Mi 7:3: Both hands are skilled in doing evil; the ruler accepts gifts, the judge takes bribes, the powerful dictate what they desire, they all*
> *conspire together.*

Can you say Supreme Court? Can you say George Bush? Can you say Koch brothers? Sure you can.

> *Ps 72:4: He will defend the afflicted among*
> *the people and save the children of the needy,*
> *he will crush the oppressor.*

Keep looking and know that it is harder to spot the good man or woman.

> *Isaiah 29:19: Oh people of Zion, who live in*
> *Jerusalem, you will weep no more. How gracious*
> *he will be when you cry for help! As soon as he hears,*
> *he will answer you.*

Sure, unless you're Palestinian. Then your cries for help will go unanswered. Your property will be taken, your land annexed, your borders blocked, food rationed, walls will be raised as a boundary between you and the Zionists. You are the one.

Brainstorming...

Isaiah 32:2 Each man will be like a shelter from the wind and refuge from the storm. Like streams of water in the desert and the shadow of a great rock in a thirsty land.

1 Ki 18:4 While Jezebel was killing off the lord's prophets, Obadiah had taken a hundred prophets and hidden them in two caves, fifty in each, and had supplied them with food and water.

Ps 55:8 I would hurry to my place of shelter, far from the tempest and the storm.

Ps 23:2 He makes me lie down in green pastures, and he leads me beside still waters.

Ps 107:35 He turned the desert into pools of water and the parched grounds into flowing springs.

Everyone needs a place to hide, or a place of rest. When the bitterness of life is overwhelming, seeking support from a friend can be the shelter that saves one's life. Just as we cannot see the wind, we also cannot see the evil planning that is going on. The spirit can be recognized through words, actions, intentions and outcomes. The tempest is just as dangerous as a lethal storm, and both can be a heap of trouble.

*Isa 35:5 Then the eyes of the blind will be opened
and the ears of the deaf unstopped.*

*Isa 42:7 To open eyes that are blind, to free the captives
from prison and to release from the dungeon
those who sit in the darkness.*

Isa 42:18 Hear, you deaf; look, you blind, and see.

*Dt 29:4 But to this day the Lord has not given you
a mind that understands or eyes that see or ears that hear.*

The deaf and blind, figuratively speaking, are captives in darkness. Those who have sight and listen are the ones released from prison, they stand in the light, and are a guide to those still in prison. The "Word" opens the eyes and ears. It is the Lord's choice to give or not to give individuals a mind that understands, eyes that see, and ears that hear.

*Isa 32:4 The mind of the rash will know and
understand, and the stammering tongue will be fluent
and clear.*

*Isa 6:10 Make the hearts of this people calloused: make their
ears dull and close their eyes. Otherwise, they might see with
their eyes, hear with their ears, understand with their hearts
and turn and be healed.*

*Isa 29:24 Those who are wayward in spirit will gain
understanding; those who complain will accept instruction.
Isa 35:6 Then the lame leap like a deer, and the
mute tongue shouts for joy.*

Even a lame tongue wants to work right. Even a lame tongue desires to shout for joy. Even a lame tongue desires to be heard. A fluent and clear tongue can make the heart of the people calloused or open.

The choice is the Lord's. Under a Kingdom of Righteousness even the mind of the rash will understand. Under a Kingdom of Righteousness, a wayward spirit comes to understand. Under a Kingdom of Righteousness, those who complain begin to accept instruction. Humbleness is raised.

The outcome produces prosperity, better fruit for the whole Kingdom. Remember, complainers don't accept instruction.

Lastly, when the hearts of the people are opened, then they understand with their hearts and are healed.

The Short Stack

The Short Stack Restaurant was a hole in the wall with no wall. A parking lot with a building. It had once been part of an industrial neighborhood under the Bong Bridge in Superior. The jobs left, the well-paying, middle-class jobs in the mills were gone. The mills were torn down, the families scattered. The streets were still there, reclaimed by weeds and scrub trees.

The mugs were old-fashioned, thick, white and heavy. The stools were covered in red Naugahyde, as were the two family booths in front of the windows. The windows looked out on desolation row, the detritus of a hundred years still blowing down the street.

Stubby and Donna Labarge owned the Short Stack. The years were in Donna's face, but not her voice. She was a caring person and it showed. Donna spoke well of people, saw the best, encouraged. But she whispered not a prayer, never said grace or "God bless you" after a sneeze. Her goodness was that of a moral person, simple as that.

On the other hand, Stubby thanked the Lord every morning when he laced up the sleeve on his prosthetic left leg, "Thank you, Lord, for letting me live. Thank you for that woman. Your word guides me every day." He struggled to straighten up. No pills today, the pain was bearable.

The couple had befriended David in a time of need. He had moved north from Tulsa, Oklahoma, to work at a group home in Ashland, east of Superior on U.S. Highway 2. But David learned a group home in Wisconsin is a different animal. At first he thought it was a better facility. But the razor wire bothered him and the uniforms were military, like those of an occupying force. The main duty of the staff was enforcement. He didn't like carrying handcuffs.

If you were a juvenile, African-American or Indian, male or female, in a four-county area of northwestern Wisconsin, Bay View was your worst nightmare. It was a priest in uniform with a nightstick and a gun. David was just too nice a guy to last. And there was that touch of schizophrenia.

He was fired for breaking a fellow staff member's arm (over his knee). The arm had been around the neck of a 14-year-old member of the Bad River Tribe. The boy was limp and his eyes had rolled up in his head when David intervened.

Snap.

The stool next to you

David had ordered one of his regular breakfasts. He had half a dozen. "Biscuits and gravy, two eggs scrambled, on the side, tomato juice." He thought the tomato juice added color.

"You want coffee?" Donna asked. She was a classic. Her face was seamed, but she smiled like she meant it. Her hair was cut at home; her husband used to cut the kids hair as well. And the dog's. A dye job would have been nice; a layer of red showed below the black and a layer of gray peeked through at the roots.

There was no mirror on the back wall of the restaurant. David looked at a coffee machine, stacks of cups and glasses, shelves of plates and bowls. A small sign read, "We grow too soon old and too late smart." It was surrounded by dried flowers.

He watched the serving window, noting the Hispanic cooks and wondered idly if they were illegal.

"Not my business," he thought.

The air changed. He heard footsteps and the creaking of a leather jacket. The stool to his right squeaked and someone sat down. Stool etiquette required space when there was none so David kept his eyes on the serving window.

The smell of roses closed his eyes. He tried to fill his head with the scent, before allowing the thought to form, waited another moment before he turned.

And she was there. Rebecca Wells watched him and said, "Hello, Mr. David."

He took in her face through the roses, tried to breathe her in, saw the changes near her eyes, but also felt the peace and strength.

"Reb," he turned his stool to face her. "I've looked for you a long time."

"But I found you."

Like the first day at the group home, she watched his face and again knew he was the one.

He started laughing. Who knows where that came from?

David looked away, then at her again, "I can still call you Reb?"

She smiled, "You gave me the name. It stuck. I liked it right off. I liked you and you gave me a nickname, what could be better. You look good, Mr. David."

He looked away.

She spoke again, "You look good, David. I'm glad I found you."

"I'm on a run to Omaha, then Denver and back home. Five days," he said.

"Philadelphia, then Atlanta," she countered. "Back in five days."

They walked to her truck. There was an older woman in the driver's seat. The woman rolled the window down, gave him a look and talked to her, "I'd say you were right, Reb. He's got a look."

She turned to him and said, "I'll bring her back. We'll meet you back here next Saturday morning at 9 a.m."

Reb climbed into the yellow Freightliner. Three red roses were stenciled on the door. Three Roses Trucking. The woman looked down at David and mouthed, "Saturday."

He listened to the yellow Freightliner go through the gears. They were headed east on Highway 2, then south through Wisconsin on Highway 51.

* * * * *

Five days. Monday morning to Saturday morning. A lot could happen. I've seen the ads on television. One moment a guy's jogging through a park and the next moment he's writhing on the ground with a heart attack. The old couple in the Cadillac cross the center line into the path of your truck. You walk down the wrong street in Milwaukee, the gang-banger picks you.

One half hour ago, I was eating breakfast, getting ready to ride. The fifth year of my quest.

It's like the grail walked in the door. I think I'm in shock. If it wasn't for the schedule on the clipboard in my hand, I would not know what to do next.

＊ ＊ ＊ ＊ ＊

He finally turned and walked to his truck, got in and situated, then put his arms on the steering wheel and his head on his arms. For over four years, he had driven steadily, taken extra runs and kept his head down. Once he had worked out a mortgage for his house and property near the Orienta Flowage, things got better. He had found his place. "North of Iron River, south of Port Wing," is all he'd say.

It was the place he called home. It provided access to Lake Superior and the Chequamegon national forests. David lived on the Iron River.

He put the Peterbilt in gear, took the Bong Bridge to Highway 23, the scenic route to Interstate 35 South. He got to thinking, which was not always a good thing, especially now.

God created Adam to be the primary predator of the earth. He gave Adam permission to name, subdue and rule over the animals. He was allowed to name his prey.

Then God thought it wasn't good for man to be alone. He made Lilith to be his wife, his primary prey. That didn't work out too well, something about being on the bottom all the time.

So God made Eve to be more compliant. I think God knew Adam would need a helper to complete his life. Does this mean woman is a better predator? Who knows, but we do know God gave man permission to leave his father and mother and unite with his wife, unite in a carnal sense. Being naked and without shame was okay.

As time went on, we see man turning God's creation of woman into prey instead of a loving wife. Just as bad, we see women becoming better predators as well.

As time went on, both men and women treated each other as predator and prey. A constructive environment, marriage, becomes destructive. There are fights and the relationship breaks down. Divorce leads to broken hearts.

"Oh, God, what am I going to do?" he thought to himself. "What was that Stone's song, *You can't always get what you want, but you get what you need.*" Something like that.

But what if you get what you want? If it's also what you need, that's one thing. What if what you want isn't what you need?

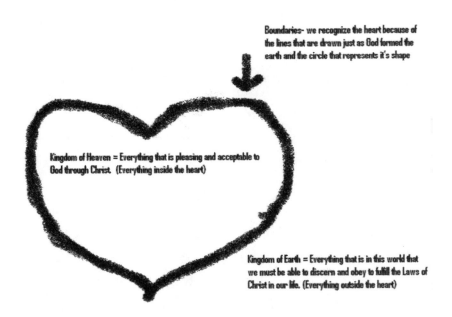

Boundaries- we recognize the heart because of the lines that are drawn just as God formed the earth and the circle that represents it's shape

Kingdom of Heaven = Everything that is pleasing and acceptable to God through Christ. (Everything inside the heart)

Kingdom of Earth = Everything that is in this world that we must be able to discern and obey to fulfill the Laws of Christ in our life. (Everything outside the heart)

What do you want, what do you need?

D avid wasn't the only one starting a trip with his head in his hands. Dolly drove. Reb forced herself to breathe. She was a believer in deep breathing. It had saved her from rash decisions and hot revenge.

They hadn't kissed. David and Reb hugged before they went to their trucks, but they didn't kiss. Never had kissed each other.

"He still smells the same," Reb thought, "I'd know his scent anywhere. Pheromones." She rode silently, thinking about David and the future. *Now what?*

She decided to stay open to the moment. Take a breath and walk through the doorway. She had dreamed all the dreams over the past five years, made pacts with the Devil and the Lord, although she didn't believe in either.

Rebecca was altruistic by nature. She held fast to stern optimism and was adept at compartmentalizing her past life, rapes in one drawer, beatings in another. But it is hard to put the future in boxes. Tomorrow was staring her in the face and she wanted to look away.

Reb and Dolly drove in silence. They turned south on Highway 51 at Hurley, took their time through Mercer, Manitowish Waters, Woodruff, Minocqua, Tomahawk and

stopped at a truck stop outside Merrill known for its Friendship House restaurant and their hamburgers.

Over coffee, Dolly asked the question, "So, my young
friend, what's next?"

"Two phrases come to mind," Reb answered.
"'Discretion is the better part of valor' and *'No guts, no glory.'* I
guess when I think about it, I haven't spent five years searching to get cold feet. It's just peculiar. One moment I'm searching and the next moment I'm found."

"Talk it out. We've got miles to go and plenty of time. Be
ready. I think the rest of your life is calling."

It's over now

So many roads to travel, some destinations known, others not on any map. Dolly and Reb went through the motions, rehearsed many times before. Now the search was over, the windmill now a real dragon. But they were not Don Quixote and his sidekick.

Two strong women had made the old Freightliner and the road their home. One had taught and the other listened, for Reb had learned about listening and Dolly loved to talk.

It wasn't supposed to work. A chance meeting in St. Paul led to a working relationship, then a strong friendship. They worked like tag-team wrestlers, always touching fingertips.

Men taunted and tried to touch, but tools were often handy and fingers broke with but a tap of the wrench. Hard slaps to the head sometimes worked.

Dolly and Reb did what it took to survive and when it wasn't needed, they were pleasant women, hard workers and good to have as friends.

In the few moments it had taken Reb to walk into the Short Stack, talk to David and walk back to the truck, it was over. Dolly had seen the change, like the handoff of the baton in a relay race. Her part in the life of Rebecca Wells was over. They both knew it and the five days together on this last road trip was both a blessing and interminable.

On the way back north, they stopped in Milwaukee and loaded Reb's old Saab into the trailer they were deadheading to Superior.

On Friday afternoon, they pulled into the terminal parking lot, unloaded the car and went through the paperwork. Then they headed to the Short Stack, Dolly in the tractor and Reb in her Saab.

Five days later. . .

D avid was early. He was sitting in one of the family booths in front of the window. He watched the women walk in. Both wore jeans and low boots. Reb wore a black leather jacket, a motorcycle jacket, well-used, over a light blue t-shirt.

Dolly walked up and introduced herself, "I'm Dolly Johnson. This is my driving partner, Reb Wells. But I guess you know each other."

"Hello, David," said Rebecca.

"Hello, Rebecca," David answered.

They sat. The waitress showed up. They ordered. Reb ordered a ham and cheese omelet with hash browns, Molly a short stack with a side of bacon and David biscuits and gravy with two eggs sunny side up on top.

Dolly laughed, "I'm going to make it easy on you two. I'm going to tell you a short story, eat some breakfast and leave. You guys can talk alone, see what's there.

"My mother beat me. She didn't do it all day, but she would haul off and sucker-punch me. She stored transgressions in her head. That's what she called them, *transgressions*. She'd whack me upside the head, then stand over me and tell me what for.

"My old man looked the other way when he noticed. But she was good and found those out-of-the-way moments.

"Enough. I was raped by a teacher, then my pastor, damn his Methodist soul. I was lucky for a while, worked at a paper mill in Brokaw, just north of Wausau, Wisconsin. Hedge fund bought the mill and it closed. I went to driving school, got propositioned by my license examiner during my final driving test. By then, I had taken a concealed carry class and joined a gun club. The driving examiner, my Glock and I had a conversation in the cab of the truck. We worked things out and I got my license.

"Fast forward to Mickey's Diner in St. Paul, Minnesota, on a Saturday morning in May a year ago. It's busy on a Saturday morning and I took the only empty stool, the one next to Rebecca. It was serendipity, kismet, fate. We talked and I offered her a future. She took it. Learns fast. She's a good driver, smart and tough."

"Three Roses?" David asked.

"There's two of us," Dolly replied, "but we let on the company is owned by my brother. A company owned by a man is less of a target."

Breakfast came.

Just the two of them

Dolly Johnson walked out of the restaurant and left David and Rebecca alone in the booth. Like the demons that rode with David, the booth wasn't really empty. They sat with desires and dreams, wants and needs, doubts and guilt.

Both had their hands on the table. David tried to fill himself with the sight of her. She placed her hand softly on his. He reciprocated and soon they had a pile of warm hands.

"I'm blessed," David said.

"Still talking to Jesus?" she asked.

"I left you in the rain." He looked down.

"It wouldn't have worked then, couldn't have." She squeezed his hands. "I picked you. Probably the first group session did it. I picked you. I watched you work with all of us. No favorites. A square deal.

"I listened to the timbre of your voice, inflections, vocabulary. You didn't simplify for the audience. I remember thinking I was going to have to look words up, use the dictionary. I love it.

"And, if you remember, I shook your hand and broke your comfort zone right off. After that, I knew what your hand felt like and how you smelled. Pheromones. I couldn't do taste that first morning in class.

"I'm sure you thought I was a wise ass. But you were the one. After that, it was patience and perseverance."

Finally, straight talk

Finally, he said to her, "Reb, I'm afraid of you. On the one hand, you are my heart's desire. But you mock my beliefs."

She thought for a moment, then replied, "Your beliefs brought us together, but love makes our future."

His brow furrowed, "But we live parallel lives."

She smiled and said, "Belly to belly and I don't give a damn."

"You make fun of everything," he said.

Rebecca looked at him, "*You asked for it.* That's what they all said about me, David. Let me tell you I have never asked for it, until now. You are the one. Pretend we're Adam and Eve if you need something biblical to justify our relationship. Even better, pretend we're Adam and Lilith, Adam's first wife. I know who I am and I don't want to be on the bottom all the time."

At the group home, she was known as Rebecca Wells. When she showed up at David's group session, she sported a Mohawk. The strip down the center was carefully cut, like the crest on a Roman helmet. Now the sides of her head were cut close, but she wasn't bald. He wanted to brush his palm over her pelt-like hair.

They stood. She put her hand on her hip, cocked her head and asked simply, "Your place?"

He laughed and looked at her, "Ride with me?"

She shook her head, "I brought my car up from Milwaukee. I need to have my own wheels. It's something I've learned. I'll follow you." So they caravanned, two heading east with a bright sun above their heads.

On the Iron River

David's forty acres was a compound, a found compound, unexpected in its symmetry. Ninety-degree angles, a square within the trees. His house was centered on his forty acres. A road had been cut through a stand of planted pine. It was a hard-packed gravel driveway.

All right, it was a cabin. Two bleached Adirondack chairs and a small table graced the wide front porch. A veranda. The cabin was two stories with two small gables balanced on either side of the centerline. There were two big windows on either side of the front door.

The wooden floors were covered with rag rugs. A big wood-framed futon with a gray and black mattress cover sat in front of one of the windows. The fireplace was blackened, well used, and big enough to cook food. A clean, large print of an old Evinrude on a small Alumacraft was centered above the mantle. Roy Rogers steered the boat. The print was signed by Roy. An old wooden clock tocked more than it ticked.

David drove, but his mind wandered.

Snap.

Corn

One incident can make a man. For David, the memory of a day in July haunts his life. His father Ray got up early that morning, intent on mowing the lawn before the Oklahoma heat set in.

The mower wouldn't start, a fouled spark plug. Ray couldn't loosen the plug. He banged his knuckles wrenching the plug from the socket. He tracked oil from the garage floor into the house and, when his wife mentioned the footprints on the rug, he head-butted her, broke her nose and then refused to take her to the emergency room.

David, then nine years old, offered to drive his mom. She cried, called a cab and they waited outside until the old Chev pulled up.

David knew emergency rooms. He had been there before with his mom. Sitting on the orange, plastic scoop chair, David thought of his grandfather's house. It had orange plastic chairs. Most of his grandfather's furniture was plastic. There was linoleum on the floors and the walls were of particle board. Furniture and clothes didn't mean much to the old man. The gun case was another matter.

David loved the smell of his grandfather's house—linseed oil and black powder, coffee and wet wool. The old man always had a gun taken apart on the kitchen table. Newspapers took the place of tablecloths. There weren't many books in the house but there were stacks of *Outdoor Life* and *True Detective*.

The old man was a farmer of sorts—grew tomatoes, potatoes, beans and corn, rows of sweet corn.

David learned to hunt with his grandfather, learned of the predator-prey relationship. His grandfather walked quietly, sat without moving, knew the habits of the deer they hunted, loaded his own ammunition.

One six-below winter morning, the old man had walked out of his house on the prairie, spied a four-point buck walking the fence line, grabbed the old Winchester 30-30 from behind the door and knocked the young buck down with one shot from the porch.

David watched from the window, then walked with his grandfather to the deer. While gutting the deer, his grandfather talked, "Grandson, today you learned the relationship between the hunter and the hunted. We do this because we love to eat deer meat. We do love to eat venison, don't we, David?"

David nodded, "Yes, Grandpa, I love deer meat." His mouth watered when he thought of a venison steak with bacon and onions.

His grandfather pulled the entrails from the young buck and stopped. "As you get older," he said, "you'll understand this, but in humanity, this is a dangerous cycle, for the prey is always the victim of the predator."

* * * * *

He looked around the emergency room. Later he would show his father the prey had turned predator. Someday David would settle the score for his mother. He would show him.

Snap.

A day in July

avid kept driving, part of the community above the road. Long-haul drivers shared characteristics. Often loners, they were self-sufficient, contained. They noticed and responded to each other.

Corn. David crossed the Mississippi at Winona and headed west across southern Minnesota. Corn and soybeans lined the highway. The spires of churches lent texture to the flatness. He liked the prairies. There were no trees clutching the sides of the roads like in northern Wisconsin. There was no topsoil up north and here the earth was rich and black.

God's bounty.

David thought of his grandfather again, went back to the farm in his thoughts. The miles accumulated. Small, white clapboard towns littered the plains, and each town had steeples. David liked the country churches even more, miles away from any community, usually set on a hill. Next to them cemeteries cradled the dead.

Corn rows surrounded the cemetery on three sides. He pulled into the parking lot of the Our Lady of Sorrows Catholic Church. He needed to shut off the truck engine and it looked peaceful here.

David took his Thermos and notebook into the cemetery, wandering the plots and reading the headstones. The plot of Steven and Mary Westerfield had a bench fashioned of steel and David sat, thanking the couple for their thoughtfulness. Years ago, cemeteries were more like parks; families often took lunches to visit relatives, or just enjoy the mown grass and shade trees.

He sipped his coffee and thought about his grandfather. The old man was gone now—no headstone, his ashes scattered along the banks of the Cimarron River in Oklahoma. David had scattered the ashes himself, talking to the old man the whole time. His family's violence did not come from the old man. His father's fury and rage were born with him, it seems.

Grandfather was spiritual, just didn't take to organized religion. He could hear his grandfather, "Believing is like a seed of corn. It grows a stalk, produces more corn on the cob. From that, there is more than enough seed corn for the earth and animals. We get our harvest, the animals eat what has fallen.

"All that growth from one little seed of corn. There is not one human can pull off what that field of corn can do. If you want to eat venison, it helps to have a little corn." With that, his grandfather laughed.

It was a good memory.

The fork in the road

He led her through the pines.

They drove east on Highway 2, north on pavement, west on gravel, and south on a dirt driveway. Over the hills and into the woods they went, he in his green 1977 Ford F-150 and she in her 20-year-old Saab two-door.

They shut off their engines and got out. Even this late in the spring, the breeze off Lake Superior was cool, but the sunshine was bright and the air was clear.

Rebecca stood and tried to take it in. She turned slowly and looked back down the driveway. She kept turning, listening to a woodpecker, and saw again the cabin that was a little more than a cabin.

David watched her, followed her gaze, looked where she did, and tried to see what she saw.

"Come in?" he asked.

"Can we walk first?"

"You bet." He gestured and hoped it seemed gallant enough for the occasion. He let her lead and they walked the property. The two-car garage was made of rough-hewn boards like the house.

The day he decided this was the place, the land he wanted, he had done what they were doing now, walked the property. David saw the four acres cut out of the surrounding forest.

Two outbuildings came with the land and house. One was larger, not quite a barn, but had two stalls for horses. He had ridden a horse once or twice. The smaller shed had a chicken coop attached, but there were no chickens. There was a dog kennel but no dog. The garden area was surrounded by an eight-foot deer fence. David had tilled, but not planted.

He took a handful of soil and looked at it. "There isn't much topsoil here on the Laurentian Plateau. The old mountains are gone and the glaciers pushed the topsoil south to Stevens Point and beyond.

"Carrots grow well here; radishes, onions, potatoes and turnips. Corn in the sun. Maybe just enough time for tomatoes. 110 days between frosts is a good year."

She took his hand and he stopped talking.

"I like to hear you talk."

Reb stood next to him and they looked back at the house. He put his arm around her shoulders. She put her arm around his waist. They stood.

He laughed again, still not knowing where that came from.

She smiled, "Feels good to me. How about coffee and you show me the house." She sighed. "I think the adrenaline of the morning has worn off."

They walked hand in hand back to the house, unsure about letting go, then entered the kitchen through the screen porch in the back. Finally, she let dropped his hand so he could make coffee. Once turned on, the old Mr. Coffee made noises. It wasn't the percolator noise of an electric coffee pot, but the smell was the same.

Rebecca looked out the window over the sink while he worked. Then he showed her the house. A living room, dining room, kitchen, small bedroom and a three-quarter bath made up the first floor. The living room ran the width of the house with stairs to the second story at one end and a stone fireplace at the other. There were two bedrooms upstairs. The master's fireplace shared a chimney with that of the living room downstairs.

The second bedroom was smaller. The upstairs bath had a large tub and shower and two sinks. Back downstairs they went.

Luckily, they both stopped thinking at the same time. He had just lit the wood in the fireplace. The pine popped and spit as the tinder caught. The warmth spread. Rebecca looked at the shoulder mount above the fireplace. David watched her and told her he had named the big buck "Wis-key" and why.

On the one hand, it was simple. She turned and gazed up at him. He bent slightly, put his hands on her shoulders and kissed her. She kissed back. It was a match made in heaven, or so he thought.

On the other hand, telling the story from a different point of view, a predator had just trapped her prey. She pulled him close.

David ached from the sweetness of the moment. He put his arms around her and smelled her hair. They kissed again, learning about each other. They worked through the five senses.

The house warmed, the afternoon cooled.

He led her to the kitchen, got down two of his favorite mugs, the ones with the bears, filled them both and gave one to her. He set cream and sugar on the table.

They were not Jack and Dianne. No way. Adam and Lilith was an apt description. David and Rebecca were going in a new direction with Jesus watching and getting a good laugh. It was said He even slapped his knee.

David looked for a sign from above, but saw only the lovely young woman across the table. He had the feeling he was going to have to figure this one out himself.

You had to give it to her. Reb had patience and, as David said, patience is needed. It's part of being a successful predator. She was willing to listen as well. Rebecca was as good a listener as David was a talker, once he got started. She prompted him by asking, "What do you think, David?"

"Well, I thank God for this moment. I thank God for the Word and his son Jesus. He leads us on a better path, a better cycle that isn't abusive or neglectful, but full of love and life. I like that. Just as there are seasons on earth, it seems that there are seasons with God.

"While the earth has spring, summer, fall and winter, God has four stages: planning, building, receiving and stewardship. In each of these stages, we see God doing something great with our lives and the lives of others.

"In the planning stage, we are able to cast a vision for the future. In the building stage, we are able to implement and execute our plans. The receiving stage allows us to inspect the quality of our decisions and decide whether it is good work or needs to be redone. Finally, we are given stewardship of the vision. We are not finished products; we must continue to grow and study the Word. In order to arrive at our destination, we must fulfill our heart's desires in Jesus Christ."

She looked at him, "Am I your heart's desire or your greatest temptation? How can we live together?"

"To live together enjoyably, we must make sacrifices and build a castle," he said, "Just as God gave the earth a form, we must form our lives with relationships. We must plan what we want it to be. We must work to make it happen and that involves sacrifice, physical, emotional and spiritual. Sacrifices allow us to stay together and enjoy our time as a couple. Tradition has it the husband's job to build the castle, provide a secure income and give instructions as to how to keep the family and the castle together."

She watched his eyes. He looked down.

She asked, "Is this what you believe? How did it work for your family?"

He was quiet for a moment, then said, "In all the days of my search, I don't think I ever thought about what it would be like to find you, the mapping of this moment. You found me. I want to throw the map away."

"Yes," she said, her face softening, "Throw the map away."

"Isaiah writes about ruling with righteousness, providing justice and shelter. He says noble men make noble plans. It involves planning, building, receiving and stewardship.

"First we plan for it. Then we build it. We receive it and watch over it. Sound familiar? In Genesis, God planned out the heavens and earth, gave the earth form, plants and animals, received it and pronounced it good and sent man to take care of the earth and his creations."

She laughed, "Define man."

"I can see this coming," David said. Then he laughed. "This is going to be *we*, isn't it?"

"You bet, Mr. David."

"Isaiah shared that when we do this correctly, we will create an environment that is peaceful, quiet and confident." David paused, "Creating this environment means secure and undisturbed homes.

He continued. "We must become disciples. This allows us to create the proper environment and relationships. This new relationship is different from the Old Testament predator versus prey relationship."

She smiled, "I like the predator end of things, having been the prey. The wolf pack seems in many ways more civilized, a structure with known boundaries and known consequences."

David reached for her hand. "Reb, I've read the Bible. I've watched the relationships of others. I've decided the best representation of my beliefs is a castle with a heart inside a castle. It's the best representation of the proper relationship between a Christian man and a Christian woman. The castle represents the proper boundaries for the family, and the heart represents the love and emotional connection the wife provides for the home. The heart is the emotional connection. Recognize His love by building a castle and recognize her love by providing protection within the walls of the castle."

"It's my turn." Rebecca took a sip of her cold coffee. "Wherever I go, I keep my own car keys, drive my own car if I want, open my own doors."

"I believe we are all equal on the circle, all equidistant from the center. It matters not your sex, color, disability or age. I think it's a Native American point of view. I'm self-educated and it's taking some time," David said.

Reb laughed. "I sure can't see this Christianity crapola. An old white guy in a beard lives above the clouds with a band of angels. He creates earth in seven days. Makes man the boss of everything, not men and women, but man. He can lord it over the earth and water, name the animals, kill what he names and eat what he kills. Then Adam comes home to a hot meal and tells old What's-her-name to turn on the television."

David looked sheepish. "That's not going to work, huh? Okay, stand up."

She stood. He walked around the table and folded her into his arms. They embraced.

"Compliant," he said, as if making a report.

Rebecca stamped her foot, pulled away and said, "Shit."

Then she looked at his face, he was smiling.

"I'm sorry," He said, still smiling, almost laughing.

"You *do* have a sense of humor." She seemed surprised.

"Laughing is as good as loving," he looked at her. "Sometimes."

"Bringing up that group home, that's taking a chance. I remember the forms, the words."

"I didn't like it either."

Dusk brought reflection. Peepers pebbled the surface of the evening. They stood on the porch, hand in hand. It seemed necessary to touch.

"Unusual," he said.

"What?" she asked

"This relationship."

"It is the damnedest thing. Do we go on from here?"

"We do. With our eyes open." They were not to stay open all night.

"We did sort of plan for this."

"Just separately. Parallel planning."

"Hungry?" he asked.

"Yes," she replied.

Darkness tucked around the trees, filled in the open spaces, gave definition to the pool of light from the oil lamp on the table. David made a fire in the wood stove, fried eggs and made toast. They ate eggs, venison sausage, pickles, toast and finished it off with vanilla ice cream and more coffee.

He held up a bottle of Seagram's and with her nod, poured a shot into each cup. They took the cups to the couch, David fed the fire and they settled in. David thought of a heart within a castle, then tried not to think and sighed.

Rebecca purred.

From dusk to dawn

Like new lovers anywhere, they made their way. The cabin that was more than a cabin took on the glow of a home.

Laughter bubbled unexpectedly. When she brought in her black nylon bag, he showed her the spare bedroom. She looked him in the eye and they laughed.

She wanted to take a shower. He showed her where the towels were kept and said he'd take one downstairs. They looked at each other and laughed.

David and Rebecca ran the hot water cold, learning of each other. Belly to belly, side to side, back to back, and cheek to cheek. They went to bed smelling of Ivory soap. Moonlight slanted through the bedroom window.

Later, surfacing, he could hear her breathing beside him, long, slow and deep. Back under he went.

Memories, dreams, came to him like frames from a black and white film. Why are memories black and white? Had he just noticed or was this new? He had never thought about it before, in all his days of remembering. The frames slid by slowly. He saw freeway on ramps, his truck.

David remembered truck stops, parking lots, tractors idling all in a row. He remembered handing out sandwiches and bottles of water from the last Kwik Trip.

Always looking.

He came to the surface again, felt her warmth underneath the cotton sheets and Pendleton blanket.

What kind of a message from the Lord was this? *Am I getting my just rewards? For what? The thoughts that lay behind the gauzy curtains or the deeds done with great deliberation in the dark?*

The small pink hours of the night

A round three in the morning, David got up and fed the embers in the old Monarch. It was still warm in the kitchen and the one oil lamp on the table left much of the room in shadow. Rebecca joined him.

In the small pink hours of the night, they had another conversation. They closed the doors of their past lives behind them. They were a couple who knew too much and the knowledge needed metal boxes, a gun cabinet of the mind. Lockable.

The conversation walked of its own volition, with heavy steps, picking places, stopping for sighs. Violations were admitted, pain spilled into words with tears. Hands rested on arms, arms around shoulders, cheeks were stroked and fingertips touched lips to silence, finally.

They closed the doors behind them, checked each room, walked the hallways, listened and smelled again the longing and the damage done.

That's all they could do, close the doors. No locks would work. But it was deliberately done, eyes wide open for it's all in the eyes.

Rebecca quoted proverbs. "Instruct a wise man, and he becomes still wiser; teach a just man, and he advances in learning."

David laughed. They were making a deal, David and Rebecca. Not Adam and Eve, Adam and Lilith. It was going to be different. It had to be.

Riding shotgun

On their first Sunday together, they drove David's pickup to town. They bought seeds—radishes, onions, potatoes, lettuce and corn. Tomato plants and metal cages went in the bed of the truck with bags of fertilizer. Groceries were next.

Sunday afternoon Rebecca and David planted corn. David told stories of his grandfather. They posed at the end of their work, like some ersatz Grant Wood painting.

David grilled hamburgers for dinner and they drank beer on the back porch. Later they packed.

Monday morning saw them in Superior. There was paperwork to fill out and arrangements to make. By one o'clock, they were ready to roll. Ten days, out and back.

They took the Bong Bridge to Highway 23 out of Duluth. It was a pretty road; the sun was bright and high. David drove and Reb rode shotgun. The demons that rode with David made room for Rebecca.

It must be said about these two travelers, once in the same moment together, they stayed there. The moment was to last many years. It is one thing to search, another to know when it is found.

Acknowledgments

Thanks to J.D. Anderson, the ultimate long-haul trucker, for his help.

And thanks to Tony and Laura Francis, Doug Boling, Terrance Terrell, Ernest Lynch, Nicolas Washington, and Marcus Evans.

About the Authors

David Seila

David Seila grew up in a small town called Inola, Oklahoma. He went into the U.S. Navy after high school and rose to the rank of Gunner's Mate. After his stint in the military, he earned a degree in Business Management from Oklahoma State University.

David began counseling after going through life-altering circumstances in his early twenties. He says he is still alive because of the counseling. He ended up going to work for a group home and used what he had learned on some of the kids. Today, he feels he would have been better off with a degree in psychology, but hindsight is often 20/20.

After four years at the group home, he asked himself what he should do with the rest of his life. He made a list, packed his bags and started his life over in Northern Wisconsin, where he decided to make a habit of outdoor adventures and activities. He took a leap of faith and is living the rest of his life a day at a time.

Michael Skubal

Mike Skubal was born in Chicago at the end of World War II. His parents were both from Rhinelander, Wisconsin, and returned there after the war. He graduated from Rhinelander High School, received a BA in Creative Communication from the University of Wisconsin–Green Bay, and a Master of Arts in Liberal Studies from Hamline University in St. Paul, Minnesota.

An actor for many years, both in Seattle and the twin cities of Minneapolis and St. Paul, Minnesota, he turned to directing, then to writing, ghostwriting, and working as a reporter and columnist for the old Rhinelander *Daily News*. He considers himself a storyteller.

The authors can be contacted at their website:
www.hodagwriters.com

CPSIA information can be obtained at www.ICGtesting.com
Printed in the USA
BVOW02*1531111016

464689BV00003B/6/P